# The
# C

Count Alucard remained for the moment where he was. He waited until the puffs and grunts from the old lady on the zimmer frame had faded away on the upper stairs. Then, gently, he lifted a branch of the Christmas tree with a forefinger, lowering a second branch with his other hand. He peered out through the space he had made, into the foyer. There was not a soul to be seen.

"Ah . . . CHOO!" At long last, the Count was able to allow himself the luxury of a noisy sneeze. The baubles on the Christmas tree rattled against each other.

Then, feeling better, Count Alucard stepped out from his hiding place and strode on his long, thin legs across the foyer and towards the revolving doors.

*Also by Willis Hall in Red Fox:*

The Last Vampire
The Vampire's Holiday
The Vampire's Revenge
Henry Hollins and the Dinosaur
The Inflatable Shop
Dragon Days
Return of the Antelope
The Antelope Company Ashore

# THE
# VAMPIRE'S
# CHRISTMAS

## Willis Hall
*Illustrations by Tony Ross*

RED FOX

A Red Fox Book
Published by Random House Children's Books
20 Vauxhall Bridge Road, London SW1V 2SA

A division of Random House UK Ltd
London Melbourne Sydney Auckland
Johannesburg and agencies throughout the world

1 3 5 7 9 10 8 6 4 2

First published by The Bodley Head Children's
Books 1994

Red Fox edition 1995

Printed and bound in Great Britain by
The Guernsey Press Co Ltd, Vale, Guernsey, C.I.

RANDOM HOUSE UK Limited Reg. No. 954009

ISBN 0 09 935691 0

# The Vampire's Christmas

# 1

*The vampire bat hovered over the snow-tipped tops of the fir trees and then swooped, out of the starlit sky, and settled on the gaunt, grey castle's ivy-covered walls. The nocturnal creature's evil eyes twinkled in the new moon's light as it fluttered its way, with the aid of bat's wing claws, along the stonework ledge beneath the upper-storey leaded casement-window. The tall window, already ajar, swung open wide with barely a creak as the vampire bat pressed its sleekly furry body against the glass. The creature shuffled its claws onto the stone window ledge and was transformed, instantly, into the human form of Count Dracula, its outstretched leathery wings becoming the wicked monster's wide-spread black cloak.*

*Inside the vaulted bedchamber, shadows danced on the stone walls from the flames of the log fire burning in the arched fireplace. Count Dracula sprang down onto the carpeted floor as lightly as any one of the snowflakes falling on the outside window ledge. The young woman who lay fast asleep in the four-poster bed, her face framed in her golden hair on the lace-edged monogrammed pillow, was unaware of the terrible fate which was about to befall her. In two quick strides the vampire count had crossed the room and his shadow* fell across the sleeping figure. Dracula's thin red lips parted and his darting tongue flickered hungrily over his two pointy needle-sharp teeth.

"*Blood – I must have blood!*" murmured the vampire to himself. "*I thirst for blood,*" he added, his mouth opening wide as, savouring each moment, he slowly lowered his teeth onto the girl's slim neck.

CLICK!

"That's quite enough of that!" Count Alucard told himself as he pressed the "Off" button on the programme-changer and the television in the corner of his hotel room went blank. "Why do they always show old horror movies at bedtime?" the real-life vampire count asked himself, with a distasteful shudder. "Now I shan't get a wink of sleep all night."

Sleeping through the hours of darkness did not come easily to Count Alucard at the best of times. It is normal vampire practice, as everyone knows, to sleep by day and to prowl by night. But Count Alucard was no normal vampire – he was the very last living member of the famous vampire aristocracy for one thing, which made life hard. He was also a vegetarian vampire, which made life even harder. For try as he would to convince folk that he was a gentle soul who would not harm so much as a fly, most people were inclined to take to their heels when they discovered his true identity. More than that, they were likely to take up sticks and stones and drive the poor chap out of their village or town.

And if the human race in general was hard on the vegetarian vampire, there were also other pinpricks

2

that made life more difficult for him than for the human race.

It really wasn't fair. Take garlic as a case in point. Like all of the vampires that had gone before him, Count Alucard hated garlic. If one single clove of the dreaded root came anywhere near him, Count Alucard was reduced to a quivering, shivering nervous wreck. Which made things difficult for him whenever he was in a restaurant. There was no problem as far as his own meal was concerned: all he needed to do was see to it that he did not order anything containing garlic. But he was so allergic to the awful stuff, that it only needed a waiter to serve up a garlicky meal to a diner at a nearby table, and the poor Count would be forced to leap to his feet and skedaddle out of the restaurant. Because of this, the Count had got into the habit of eating either in fast-food joints or transport cafés.

Best of all, when he was staying in a hotel – as he was now – he made sure that he took all of his meals in his room.

"Is that room-service?" the Count said into the telephone, fancying a late-night snack to chase away the horrors of the horror movie he had switched on by mistake.

"It is indeed, sir. How can I be of assistance?"

"This is room 613 – I was wondering if you might consider it an impertinence, at this late hour, were I to ask if you would furnish me with a cheese salad and a glass of cold milk?"

"Not at all, sir!" said the cheerful voice on the other end of the telephone. "We provide a twenty-four hour service. I shall attend to it immediately.

It will be my pleasure, sir."

"How kind of him," the Count murmured to himself as he replaced his bedside telephone and laid his head back on the pillows he had plumped up on the bed. He had already changed into his pyjamas over which he wore his black silk dressing-gown which had a scarlet collar and the letters C.A. embroidered, also in scarlet, on the breast pocket. "But then again," he told himself sadly, "I don't suppose he would have been quite so obliging had he known that it was a vampire's needs to which he was attending."

No, the Count continued ruminating to himself, there were few folk on this earth who were inclined to look upon him kindly when they knew who he was. Except, of course, for Henry Hollins.

Henry Hollins was a twelve-year-old schoolboy whom Count Alucard had had the rare good fortune to come across on two occasions. He had met him for the first time in the Count's native Transylvania, when Henry had been on holiday there with his parents. The Count had come across Henry for a second time in Scarcombe, an English seaside town where the Hollinses had again been on holiday. On both of these occasions, the Count had had good reason to be grateful to Henry who had stood by him when he had found himself harassed by the local authority and hounded by local townsfolk. Henry Hollins was one of the few friends – perhaps the *only* friend – that Count Alucard could count upon in times of trouble.

"I wish I knew where Henry was," the Count murmured to himself, his sad, dark eyes roaming round the close confines of his hotel bedroom. But on both of their previous encounters, Count Alucard and Henry Hollins had been caught up in such exciting, time-consuming adventures, that they had never paused to give a moment's thought to exchanging addresses or telephone numbers. Count Alucard had no idea where, or how, he might get in touch with Henry Hollins.

Not that this would have worried him unduly under normal circumstances. Ordinarily, the Count was more than happy with his own company. Count Alucard was a loner who found enjoyment mostly in solitary pursuits. He enjoyed walking – either through the snow-covered forests of his Transylvanian homeland, or strolling in the English countryside. He liked music – and would sit for hours with his ancient gramophone and his collection of old records. He loved reading – and was never happier than when he was curled up in front of a roaring fire, a glass of tomato juice laced with Worcester sauce at his elbow, thumbing through the pages of his favourite magazine, *The Coffin-Maker's Journal*, looking at the coloured pictures of examples of that craftsman's art.

But this was no normal circumstance. Count Alucard pulled a doleful face. There was less than a week to go to Christmas and there was not one single Christmas card on his hotel room dressing-table. Even worse, he was faced with the prospect of spending that holiday on his own, with no one to exchange a present with or wish "A Very Merry Xmas!"

Downstairs in the hotel's foyer and next to the giant-sized Christmas tree, was a stand on which there was displayed the menu for the Christmas Day lunch: a five-star, five-course feast complete with crackers, poppers and all of those other good things that go with Christmas. But what good is a Christmas cracker without a friend on its other end? And how much enjoyment can be had from a Christmas dinner, when it is taken at a "table for one"?

Count Alucard's gloomy ponderings were inter-rupted by a knock on the door. A moment later, the affable waiter who had taken his order on the telephone, was standing in the room.

"Good evening again to you, sir! And where would you like it?" said the waiter, indicating the silver tray which he was holding, shoulder-high and balanced on the upturned, outstretched fingers and thumb of one hand. "How's-about the dressing-table?"

"That would be exceedingly kind of you," replied the Count, swinging his legs from off the bed and slipping his bare feet into his black velvet slippers which were embroidered with the same C.A. monogram as his dressing gown.

"There we are then, sir! One glass of ice-cold milk and a nice cheesey salad!" As he spoke, the waiter lifted the silver cover from off the plate of food then added, proudly: "How does that look to you? Speaking personally, I can't remember ever seeing a nicer looking salad than that!"

But something, it seemed, as far as the Count was concerned, was definitely amiss. His long, thin fingers twitched nervously at the collar of his dressing-gown while a worried frown creased his high, pale forehead. He cleared his throat, quickly, several times.

"Anything the matter, sir?" queried the waiter, noting the Count's concern.

"You wouldn't happen to know, by any chance, the ingredients contained in that salad dressing?"

"Indeed I would, sir," said the waiter, proudly. "The chef went off duty at ten o'clock so I made that salad dressing with my own fair hands. I don't intend to stay a waiter all my life – I'm doing a course in cookery at night school. Let me see

7

now . . .?" As he continued, the waiter ticked off, on his fingers, the items he had put into the dressing: "Olive oil; malt vinegar; a dash of pepper; a squeeze of garlic; a hint of lemon juice—"

But the vegetarian vampire was not listening – he was not even in the room. Before the waiter could complete his recitation of the salad dressing's contents, the Count had sprung across the room, flung open the door and taken off at full speed.

"Well I never!" murmured the waiter, puzzled. "I wonder what it was I said that upset the gentleman?"

Count Alucard sprinted along the corridor as fast as his long, thin, legs would carry him, anxious only to put as much distance between himself and the obnoxious stench of garlic as was possible. Not pausing to wait for the lift, the vegetarian vampire raced down the main staircase and into the hotel's impressive foyer. An American couple who had just returned to the hotel after an evening's theatre-going, wining and dining, paused to stare in open-mouthed astonishment at the curious sight of the long-limbed figure speeding across the marbled floor, his dressing-gown cords streaming out behind him. Arriving at the hotel's entrance, the Count pushed hard on the plate-glass revolving doors which spun round, depositing him outside on the moonlit forecourt.

Only then, with the December chill night air biting through his thin pyjamas, did the Count pause to consider what he had done. What was worse, in his headlong flight he had lost one of his velvet slippers and the ground beneath his one bare foot was not only cold but damp. Why was it, he wondered, that garlic had such an effect not only upon himself, but upon all vampires? Why was he unable to bite back his revulsion for that dreadful root?

But this was not the time to ponder on such matters, he told himself, as he hopped on his slippered foot into the hiding place he had chosen behind a potted shrub on the forecourt. What was more important was for him to decide upon his next move. He could not go back into the hotel without being called upon to give embarrassing explanations – perhaps even having to reveal his true identity. On the other hand, he could hardly spend the night out in London's West End thoroughfares, wearing a dressing-gown, pyjamas, and minus a slipper. There was only one thing for it, he decided. He would vanish into the night in the same manner as his vampire predecessors had sought escape throughout the centuries. He would turn into a bat.

Taking hold of his dressing-gown's hem, in either hand, and spreading it wide as if it was a cloak, the Count lifted his face towards the moon, took a deep breath, and launched himself into the air. The effect was instantaneous. The hotel's commissionaire, returning to his post by the entrance after seeing off a departing guest in a taxi, was suddenly frozen stiff with fear as a dark, furry creature swept past him on widespread wings, almost brushing the tip of his nose before fluttering upwards into the night sky.

Back in the hotel foyer, the two American tourists,

having collected their room key from reception, crossed towards the main staircase. They paused, *en route*, and the husband stooped to pick up an object off the floor near the Christmas tree.

"I'll be a monkey's uncle, Miriam," observed the tourist to his wife, turning the black velvet monogrammed slipper over in his hand. "The dude that dashed out a moment ago left half his footwear behind."

"Land sakes, Cyrus," gasped the lady tourist. "Just like Cinderella!"

"May I see that, sir?" said a voice from over their shoulders. Turning round, the tourists saw that the voice had come from a round-faced, balding man who was wearing a navy-blue suit, brown boots, a shirt which seemed a shade tight on him, and a navy-blue tie which had a pair of crossed truncheons embroidered on it. His name was Howard Dobson. He was an ex-detective sergeant and he was now employed as the hotel's security officer.


"That *is* odd!" observed Mrs Hollins to her husband. She was standing by the sideboard, which was decorated with Christmas cards and holding two of them, one in each hand, at arms' length as she squinted at them each in turn.

"What's that, Emily?" asked Albert Hollins, dipping a digestive biscuit into his bedtime mug of cocoa.

"Well, this," said Emily, waving one of the cards in her husband's direction. "You see this one that came today – with the Three Wise Men sitting on

11

their camels looking up at the bright star – the one we got from your Uncle Sumner?"

"What about it?"

"It's the dead spitting image of the card we got last year from that nice couple we met on holiday, in Scarcombe, two summers ago."

"Well, I never," replied Albert Hollins, sounding not over-impressed as he added: "Wonders will never cease."

"Ah, but there's more to come," continued Emily, turning the other card towards Albert. "This one, with the little robin sitting on the Yuletide log – the one we got from the Scarcombe couple – it's the exact double of the one we got last year from your Uncle Sumner. Isn't that amazing?"

"How do you know?"

"I remember it."

"Nobody remembers things like that," said Mr Hollins.

"I do," said Emily Hollins, proudly, adding: "very clearly."

Mr Hollins made no reply. Not because he had no wish to take the argument further – but for the reason that a much more serious matter had come to his attention. Glancing down into his mug, he had realised that a large part of his digestive biscuit had broken off and was now floating in his cocoa. As he watched, glumly, and before he could put in his forefinger and thumb to lift out the half-circle of soggy biscuit, it upended, rather like the *Titanic*, sank out of sight beneath the cocoa's murky surface and then reappeared, disintegrating in front of his eyes.

"I don't know about you, Emily," said Albert with a sigh, rising to his feet, "but I'm calling it a day."

Emily Hollins replaced the Christmas cards on the sideboard among their fellows, readjusted the luminous, plastic angel which was doing a passable imitation of The Leaning Tower of Pisa on the top of the Christmas tree, and switched out the light as she followed her husband out of the living-room.

As Emily and Albert arrived upstairs on the landing, their son Henry, called out to them: "Goodnight, Dad! Goodnight Mum!"

"Nighty-night, Henry!" his father called back, jocularly. "Don't let the bed-bugs bite!"

"Goodnight, Henry – try and go to sleep!" called Emily, adding: "Christmas is coming – you need all the sleep you can get!"

But it was thoughts of Christmas that were keeping Henry awake. He was finding sleep hard to come by as he gazed out at the moonlit sky through a chink in the curtains. It was not his own holiday arrangements that were causing Henry concern. Christmas at the Hollins' home was always a joyous family affair, despite its minor mishaps.

Last year, for instance, Emily Hollins had managed to drop the turkey as she lifted it out of the oven – and it had shot across the kitchen floor, frightening the cat which had leapt up onto the table, knocking over the bowl of sprouts, sending them bouncing around the room. Then, when they had completed their main course, Albert's shoe-heel had skidded in a patch of turkey grease which,

13

despite all of Emily's brisk efforts with mop and bucket, had stubbornly stayed behind on the kitchen flooring. Albert had not only been completely upended, he had also come down, elbow first, in the bowl of custard which had been intended for the Christmas pudding.

But it was not incidents such as those that were causing Henry to lose his sleep. Such mishaps, after all, provide the very stuff from which the magic fabric of family Christmases is woven. No, he was worrying about his old friend, Count Alucard, and wondering how and where the vegetarian vampire would be spending Christmas.

The boy knew that the Transylvanian Count had been driven out of his native land by ignorant, unthinking folk who refused to recognise what was crystal clear for all to see: that the last of the vampires was a kind and gentle person. Not only that, but Henry was also aware that cruelty and ignorance were not only to be found in Transylvania, but all around the world. The Count had travelled widely in his search for a quiet life and a little understanding, and had been unwelcome wherever he had shown his face.

"Wherever you are, I hope you have a very Happy Christmas," murmured Henry to his absent friend, as he looked out through the chink in the curtains at the black velvet sky which was rich with stars. "I wish that I could see you again," he added.

Henry thumped his pillow into shape and then nestled his head against it – unaware that, particularly at Christmastime, the most improbable of wishes are sometimes granted.

14

It occurred to the Count that there could be few
better ways of looking at London, than the one in
which he was viewing it now: hanging upside-down
from the topmost point of one of the high girders
of Tower Bridge. It was a calm clear night and,
had he so desired, he could have counted the bob-
bing stars reflected in the river below. There were
lights coming from the boats moored all along the
Embankment – and from the floodlit city beyond,
stretching away off into the distant, twinkling suburbs, as far as a keen bat's eye could see.

When morning came, the Count decided, he
would have to return to the hotel and hope to
somehow get back inside his room unnoticed – but
for now, he was happy enough to hang suspended,
his sharp claws clutching the iron girder, his black
wings wrapped around his furry body, keeping him
snug and warm despite the chill December night.

15

Somewhere, off in the distance, a tug's hooter let out a mournful wail. The vegetarian vampire's eyelids drooped over his bright, black eyes and he fell fast asleep.

Some several hundred miles away, in the back bedroom of No. 42 Nicholas Nickleby Close, in the northern market town of Staplewood, Henry Hollins was also fast asleep at last.

# 2

The vegetarian vampire's agitation was increasing by the second as he fluttered along the hotel's outside walls. It was still quite dark and, at this early hour, one hotel-room window looked very much like the next, particularly as with most of the hotel's occupants still abed, most of the window curtains were still closed.

The Count had decided, almost an hour before, that it would be foolish to wait for dawn before setting out in search of his hotel. Unwrapping his parchment-like wings from around his body, he had loosened his claw-hold on the Tower Bridge girder and flown off, scudding first across the river and then gaining height to skim over the roof of the Houses of Parliament, cruising past Big Ben. Locating his hotel had proved an easy task – his bat's unerring sense of direction had instinctively guided him the right way. Once in the general area, he had recognised the hotel instantly, despite the cloud cover and darkness, from overhead.

But finding his hotel room was proving an altogether more difficult task. To add to his confusion, almost all of the windows had been left open – it was the hotel's policy to keep the central heating system turned full on during the winter months.

He could, of course, have eased his way in through any one of the curtained windows, if only to get his bearings. But above all else, the Count prided himself on being a courteous man – he did not dare to imagine what effect his presence might cause some elderly lady-guest, were she to wake and find a sharp-toothed, beady-eyed vampire bat circling over her bed!

The solution suddenly occurred to him. Of course! So simple! Why hadn't he thought of it before? He had just remembered that the Fire Escape was situated next to Room 620. He was in Room 613. If he counted seven windows along from the Fire Escape, he would be home and dry.

Moments later he was pushing his snub nose through the curtains. Yes! It was his room! There was his glass of milk, untouched, on the dressing-table. There was the disgusting plate of salad, drenched in garlic – thank goodness that the waiter had replaced the cover before going out of the room. The vegetarian vampire's furry body shivered with distaste. His black, beady eyes peered further into the room. He could see his copy of the *Coffin Maker's Journal* on the bed where he had left it, lying open at the double-page picture showing the inviting satin-lined Excalibur model, lined with red satin and sporting four Gothic-style silver-plated handles. What wouldn't he give for a good night's sleep in one of those . . .?

Shrouding his wings, the Count eased the rest of his bat's body through the curtains, rested for a moment on the metal frame of the windowsill and then sprang lightly into the room. Instantly, he was Count Alucard, the man, again. Back in his striped pyjamas and his black silk monogrammed dressing-gown, one foot slippered, one foot not. He rubbed his bare foot on the carpet, feeling the warmth of the pile beneath his toes. Hanging upside-down from Tower Bridge had been an adventure he had savoured, but it was good to get back to five-star comfort and the safety of his hotel room, his adventuring behind him.

"And a very good morning to you, sir – I trust you enjoyed your night out?"

The Count jumped with surprise – the voice had seemed to come from nowhere. Then the wardrobe door was pushed open from inside and a short, stout man in a navy-blue suit and wearing a tie that was embroidered with crossed truncheons stepped into the room.

"Who are you?" said the Count, quickly recovering himself and angry at the unwarranted intrusion. "And what were you doing in my wardrobe?"

"I believe these belong to you, sir," said the intruder, ignoring the Count's protestations then, flinging open the wardrobe door again, he listed the items of clothing hanging on the coat hangers: "One black dinner jacket with matching trousers; one white dress shirt; one black bow tie; a black cloak lined with scarlet."

"What about them?" said the Count.

"What about *you*? Out all night on the town – coming back, before it's light, through a sixth floor window. I've got your number, my lad. You're a blood-drinking vampire, aren't you?"

"No, I'm not!" The Count denied the charge, stoutly.

"Oh, yes you are! Don't try to tell me different. My name is Howard Dobson. I'm the hotel's security officer. I spotted you nipping out through the revolving doors late last night in your dressing-gown and jim-jams. I know a scary monster when I see one."

"But I've already told you: I'm *not* a scary monster."

"Don't give me that!" snapped Howard Dobson. "I've checked you out, matey. I've looked you up in the hotel register. You're booked in as Count Alucard – any idiot could work out that 'Alucard' is 'Dracula' spelled backwards. I didn't spend twenty years as a detective sergeant for nothing."

"All right, my name *is* Alucard," said the Count. "But I give you my word that I'm not what you think I am. As a matter of fact, I'm a vegetarian."

"Oh, yes," sneered the security officer, "and I'm the Emperor Napoleon! I'll tell you something else: we don't take kindly to guests who go round sticking their pointy fangs into other guests and sucking out all their blood. That's not the kind of thing that gets a posh hotel like this a good name – particularly when it's close to Christmas."

"I have not stuck my 'pointy fangs', as you see fit to call them, into anyone," replied the Count, stiffly, then drawing himself up to his full, gangly height, he added: "I wouldn't."

"Not yet, you haven't – but only because you realised I was onto you," retorted Dobson. "Do you want me to spell it out for you? Shall I show you how I can prove, beyond a shadow of doubt, that you're a vampire through and through?" As he spoke, the security officer crossed to the dressing-table and allowed one hand to hover over the previous night's supper tray. "Vampires can't stand garlic, can they? That's a well-known fact. Shall I lift the lid off this cheese salad and see what a whiff of garlic does to you?"

"No! Please – no!" Count Alucard swallowed hastily and his long, pale hands fluttered in the air. "I'll do anything . . ."

"I think that proves my point," said Dobson, smugly. "I worked the whole thing out last night, you see, after I questioned the night waiter. Righty-ho, then Drac. We'll pop along and see the hotel manager, shall we? And see what he has to say about it?"

"May I be allowed to put some clothes on first?"

"Be my guest," replied the ex-detective with a smile, happy to be obliging in his victory.


Roland Rennishaw, the hotel manager, leaned forward, resting his elbows on his desk, and gazed gravely through his gold-rimmed glasses, first at his security officer and then at the tall, thin, pale-faced, black-cloaked, dinner-jacketed guest that Dobson had brought in with him.

"I hope you've got your facts right, Dobson," said the hotel manager. "These are very serious accusations."

"Oh, absolutely, sir!" replied the security officer.

"He's a blood-drinking vampire without a shadow of a doubt. I shouldn't let him come near you either – he'll sink those pointy fangs into your neck before you can say 'Transylvania'!"

"I wouldn't dream of doing anything so utterly uncouth," murmured the Count with a distasteful grimace. "I'm a strict vegetarian – as I've already attempted to explain to this gentleman, but he refuses to listen."

The hotel manager sighed and tugged at his neatly trimmed moustache with thumb and forefinger – a sure sign that he was thinking hard.

But the real truth of the matter was that Roland Rennishaw didn't really know *what* to think. The man standing on the opposite side of his desk certainly *looked* and dressed like a vampire, from his sleek, combed-back hair down to the tips of his shiny-black patent leather shoes. On the other hand, Dobson's judgement was not always to be trusted. The security officer was inclined to take his duties much too seriously. He was constantly accusing hotel guests of having committed some misdemeanour or another. And when he wasn't finding fault with the hotel's visitors, he was carping and complaining at their children. He growled at them for running up and down the main staircase; he grumbled at them for joy-riding in the lifts. Why, only a couple of nights before, he had reduced one poor little girl to tears, simply for touching the baubles on the Christmas tree in the foyer. In fact, it seemed to the hotel manager, that his security officer would have been better suited to employment in a top security prison, rather than a five-star hotel. Roland Rennishaw sighed again as he watched Dobson flick open his notebook and begin to read what he had written down.

"Whilst in the pursuance of my official duties," began the security officer, having noisily cleared his throat, "on the night of Wednesday, the 19th of December, I had occasion to enter the foyer, where I observed the accused, Count Alucrad—"

"My name is Count Alu*card*," broke in that gentleman.

The security officer frowned, screwed up his eyes and squinted at what was written in his notebook. "Sorry, I must have written it down wrong," he said, taking a pencil with an eraser on one end out of his pocket and rubbing at his notebook, hard. Then, turning the pencil round, Dobson corrected his mistake and continued: "—where I observed the accused, Count Alu*card*, dressed in an improper fashion and behaving in a suspicious manner . . ."

But the hotel manager wasn't listening. He knew, from past experience, that Dobson's reciting of his evidence was going to take some time – it always did! And time was a commodity which the hotel manager did not have to spare. He had to decide – and quickly – on the course of action he was going to take. It was a difficult decision to make and he was angry with his security officer for putting him in this awkward position.

Rennishaw, a kindly man by nature, was inclined to believe Count Alucard's side of the story. He tended to accept that the vampire *was* a vegetarian and therefore provided no threat to the other hotel residents. After all, the Count had been staying in the hotel for over a week and there had been no complaints, so far, about him having bitten – or even nibbled – anybody. There was nothing in the hotel's Complaints Book to say that the Count had frightened anyone in the slightest way. On the other hand, when it came to frightening visitors, the hotel manager reminded himself, it was his security officer, Howard Dobson, who led the field in that account. Take the business of the little girl and the Christmas tree as a case in point.

But even if the Count *was* telling the truth and he was entirely harmless – would it still be wise to allow him to remain in the hotel as a guest? How would the other residents react, the hotel manager wondered, if word got around that they would be spending Christmas in the company of a Transylvanian vampire count? Half of them would check out immediately, the manager guessed, while the others would lock themselves inside their bedrooms for the entire holiday. And what sort of a Christmas would the hotel celebrate then, the hotel manager wondered, gloomily?

This year's Christmas-Eve Party Get-Together, scheduled for 6 p.m. in the Main Lounge and intended for the guests to get to know one another, would go unattended. The mince pies would stand untouched. Tray upon tray of glasses filled with medium-sweet sherry or orange juice would remain ignored. The yearly carol service, due to take place in the Coffee Room, also on Christmas Eve, would go unsung. And how would his waiters feel, the hotel manager wondered, if they were asked to deliver each and every De Luxe Christmas Day Dinner (as proudly advertised on the wooden stand in the hotel foyer: melon balls or prawn cocktail; roast turkey, chipolata sausages, bread sauce, sage-and-onion stuffing, *dauphinoise* potatoes, buttered carrots, Brussel sprouts, followed by Christmas pudding with brandy butter – rounded off with coffee and after-dinner mint chocolates wrapped in gold foil) – on individual trays to the occupants cowering in their rooms? The vast dining-room, which had been carefully decorated by the hotel staff with rows of silver bells and sprigs of holly, would stand empty all Christmas Day long. It would not resound, as in previous years, with joyful laughter and the snap-snap of pulled Christmas-crackers. It would be silent and dull and deadly dreary. It would be like spending Christmas on board the *Marie Celeste*.

The hotel manager frowned as he glanced across at his security officer who was still reeling off the evidence contained in his notebook.

". . . Acting upon information received," Dobson droned on in his best ex-policeman's boring tones, "and without giving a moment's thought to my personal safety, I decided to secrete myself inside the wardrobe of Room 613 and await further developments . . ."

Rennishaw's frown deepened as his attention was drawn elsewhere. Something was happening outside the hotel. He could hear the sounds of raised, angry voices as they drifted up from the forecourt.

Count Alucard had heard them too, growing louder by the second. Edging closer to the window, he eased himself up onto tiptoe and glanced down. What he saw caused him to gulp, hastily. For it was the kind of scene he had encountered on many previous occasions, in different countries all around the world.

A crowd, consisting of some thirty to forty hotel guests and members of staff, was milling on the forecourt. Many of them carried makeshift weapons. Several of the guests had armed themselves with billiard cues from the Games Room. A red-faced chef, wearing a chef's white hat and coat and chef's blue-and-white check linen trousers, was brandishing a meat cleaver which glistened in the early morning sunlight. Some guests were waving walking sticks and umbrellas. One old lady, whose gnarled hands gripped the handles of her

26

zimmer frame, managed to lift it above her head where she shook it, angrily, for several seconds before lowering it back to the ground. A thick-set waiter was holding aloft the wooden menu from the hotel's foyer, while the Christmas Day menu it had once contained was being trampled underfoot.

Count Alucard's sharp ears could also make out the cries that were coming up from the crowd below: "Death to the Vampire!" they shouted, and "Down with Dracula!"

There were newspapermen standing on the edge of the crowd, some with cameras at the ready, others with ballpoint pens poised over open notebooks. Some workmen were unloading equipment from out of a big white van which had: "BBC Television – Outside Broadcasts" printed in green letters across its side. A young lady newscaster, whose name was Linda Lewington, was making last-minute adjustments to her make-up as she prepared to face the TV cameras.

"The news has spread quickly," the vegetarian vampire murmured to himself as he gazed down sadly at the activity outside. But then, as the Count had come to realise all too often and to his cost, it never did take very long for news of his arrival to spread through any neighbourhood.

It was, of course, Howard Dobson who had let the cat out of the bag. The security officer was quite unable to keep any secret to himself. Having first decided not to breathe his suspicions of a vampire to a living soul, he had then mentioned them, in confidence, to the very first person he had met: the hotel's night porter. The night porter,

28

having vowed that he would not say a word to anyone, had passed the secret on to a couple of Japanese tourists as they entered the hotel after a night out on the town. The two Japanese, having assured the night porter that the secret was safe with them, had gone off to the bar for a nightcap where they had promptly told the barman everything. The barman, in his turn, having told the Japanese that they could trust his absolute discretion, had passed on the disturbing news about the vampire's possible presence to every late-night customer that drifted into the bar. In this way rumour had flourished. The results of that previous night's tittle-tattling were now massed outside on the hotel's forecourt.

Count Alucard knew that it would not be long before the angry shouts outside would be replaced with actions. If he was going to escape from the wrath of the crowd, he would have to move quickly. The Count weighed up his chances. The hotel manager's attention was fixed on the forecourt. The hotel's security officer's eyes were concentrated on his notebook.

". . . At approximately 0600 hours this morning," droned Dobson, flicking over another page, "from my hiding place in the wardrobe, I was suddenly struck with the chilling fear that I was no longer alone in Room 613, despite the fact that no living human being had effected an entrance through the door . . ."

Feeling behind his back with one hand, the Count located the door knob. It turned easily at his touch and without a sound. A moment later –

without either Rennishaw or Dobson having noticed that he had gone – the Count was standing in the first floor corridor, outside the manager's office. There was no time to wait for the lift. His black, patent-leather shoes barely touched the thick pile as he skipped hastily down the broad, main staircase, keeping close to the wall so as not to be seen by anyone in the foyer. But, thankfully, the foyer was empty. All of the staff were outside with the crowd.

Miss Buttershaw, the plump lady in charge of the reception desk and normally the mildest-mannered of persons, had led the way out onto the forecourt. "Follow me!" she had cried, snatching up the long pole which was used to close the upper windows. "A curse upon all vampires!" For it is curious how a dread of vampires is tucked away inside most human beings, needing only a cloud across the moon or an unexpected footfall on a dark night, to send a shiver up the spine.

But this was broad daylight, the Count reminded himself with a little sigh, and it was very nearly Christmas – a time for peace, understanding and goodwill towards all men, and yet there was a size-able crowd gathered on the forecourt and yelling its combined head off for his downfall.

Even as he pondered upon his unhappy situation, the foyer doors burst open and the angry crowd stormed in, waving their makeshift weapons over their heads. They were led by the chef, brandishing his meat cleaver, with the old lady on the zimmer frame bringing up the rear and having some slight difficulty in negotiating her way through the revolving doors. At the same time, Count Alucard heard a door slam on the first floor landing and he realised that the hotel manager and the security officer had discovered he was no longer with them.

"This way, sir! Down the stairs!" Dobson's voice drifted down to where the Count was standing. "We'll soon catch up with him. He can't have got very far."

Hearing the approaching footsteps of the hotel's manager and its security officer at his back and with the throng of angry vampire hunters pressing into the foyer, the Count glanced nervously around in search of a hiding place. Miss Buttershaw, thrusting her window pole up at the chandeliers, in the manner of a Zulu warrior raising his spear at the sun in a tribal dance, arrived at the foot of the main staircase at the very same moment that Dobson and Rennishaw reached the bottom step.

"Didn't he come down here?" demanded Dobson.

Miss Buttershaw shook her head, firmly. "He isn't in the foyer," said that lady, firmly, gripping her window pole. "And he certainly hasn't left the hotel – we've been on the forecourt and we'd have seen him coming out."

Count Alucard, who had stepped behind the Christmas tree at the foot of the staircase, held his breath. It was a difficult thing for him to do. One of the tree's twinkling lights was tickling his nose as it flashed on and off. But the Count did not dare to move so much as a centimetre.

"He must have gone upstairs then," said the

31

Security Officer. "Perhaps he's hiding in his room. He's in 613."

"You lot go up in the lifts!" commanded Amelia Buttershaw, turning on a group of senior citizens who had been booked into the hotel on the first night of a coach tour which would take in most of the stately homes of England – though they were beginning to wish they had stayed in their own more modest homes. "The rest of you follow me!" she added, sweeping Rennishaw and Dobson along with her as she led her troops in a concerted charge up the stairs.

Count Alucard remained for the moment where he was. He waited until the puffs and grunts from the old lady on the zimmer frame had faded away on the upper stairs. Then, gently, he lifted a branch of the Christmas tree with a forefinger, lowering a second branch with his other hand. He peered out through the space he had made, into the foyer. There was not a soul to be seen.

"Ah . . . CHOO!" At long last, the Count was able to allow himself the luxury of a noisy sneeze. The baubles on the Christmas tree rattled against each other.

Then, feeling better, Count Alucard stepped out from his hiding place and strode on his long, thin legs across the foyer and towards the revolving doors.

# 3

"This won't do at all," said Albert Hollins, for the third time that morning. "I can't sit here watching the telly – it's time I was on my way to the office."

"But it's Saturday, Dad," said Henry, who was also gazing fixedly at the TV in the corner of the living-room.

"And it's very nearly Christmas," said Emily who, as if to illustrate her words was adding the several Christmas cards which had arrived that morning to the growing collection on the sideboard. "Ooooh!" she continued excitedly, "Here's a good one – it's got Santa's reindeer and his sleigh parked up on a roof that's got an attic window in it, just like your Uncle Sumner's!"

"What a coincidence," murmured Albert, who was not really listening.

"I suppose Santa must be down the chimney, dishing out toys – you can see his boot prints in the snow," said Emily. Then, returning to her original theme, she continued: "Do you *have* to go into work today, Albert? On the very last Saturday before Christmas?"

"The fact that it *is* Christmas next week is the very reason why I'm having to go into the office on

Saturday morning," said Albert with a sigh, still making no attempt to move. "We're rushed off our feet with last-minute Christmas orders."

Albert Hollins worked at the garden gnome factory which was on the outskirts of the town. This year's special Christmas offer, consisting of two gnomes (for the price of one) pulling a Christmas cracker and done up in a gift-wrapped box was proving a winner with the general public. Huge lorries, stacked to their roofs with these seasonal packages were leaving the factory every hour, on the hour, for destinations as far apart as Land's End and John O'Groats. But even though Mr Hollins knew full well that his presence was urgently required in the packing office at the Staplewood Garden Gnome Company Ltd, in order to attend to these important matters, he still found it difficult to tear himself away from the exciting events unfolding, in front of his eyes, on the news programme on the television.

"Behind one of these windows," said the voice of Linda Lewington, as the TV camera roved along the hotel's upper storeys, "lurks the evil, blood-sucking monster, waiting to sink his pointy teeth into his next unsuspecting, luckless victim . . ." The TV newscaster paused as the picture changed from the hotel to one of Linda herself, speaking into the camera. ". . . will the wicked vampire feast himself on some innocent person's blood? Or will the brave band of men and women we have watched storm inside the building, succeed in capturing him?"

"What a carry-on!" gulped Albert, softly, adding: "It certainly is nail-biting stuff, isn't it, Henry?"

But Henry Hollins did not reply. He was thinking hard. He had been wondering, ever since the programme had begun, whether the vampire in question might possibly turn out to be none other than his old friend Count Alucard, whom he had believed to be back home in Transylvania. And now, only a moment before, he had glimpsed the familiar black-cloaked, tall, long-legged figure stride out through the hotel's revolving doors, unnoticed by the TV newscaster who had turned her back on the building in order to face the camera.

"It *is* Count Alucard!" Henry murmured to himself as he watched the Count walk out of the TV camera's range of vision and into the London morning. Neither had Henry's father noticed the vampire Count's brief entrance and exit – his eyes had been firmly fixed on the TV newscaster. It occurred to Henry that he might be the only person to have realised that the Transylvanian vampire Count was no longer trapped inside the hotel. "I hope they never find him," Henry added to himself.

"What was that, Henry?" asked his father. "Did you say something?"

"No, Dad. Leastways, nothing important."

"Suffering tomcats! Just look at the time!" exclaimed Mr Hollins, glancing at his watch. "I wish I could stay and watch some more of this exciting stuff," he added, casting a last, long, lingering glance at the television, where the sound of fast-approaching sirens heralded the imminent arrival of police cars on the hotel forecourt. "But time, tide and garden gnomes wait for no man," joked Albert as he got to his feet. "Toodle-pip, Emily," he added as he headed for the door. "I'll see you both at lunchtime – provided I can get that shipment of Chrissie gnomes destined for the Shetland Islands on its way to Manchester Airport."

"Have a nice morning, Albert," said Emily Hollins, absently. She was trying to decide whether to put a card which showed a picture of a cheeky robin perched on a Christmas pudding in front of, or behind, a card which did not have a picture but was decorated, in silver-glitter lettering, with the simple message: A HAPPY CHRISTMAS. Emily much preferred the Christmas pudding card – the problem being that 'A HAPPY CHRISTMAS' had come from Mrs Figgins who lived next-door-but-one. Mrs Figgins might very easily pop into the Hollins' home without any warning – in which case she would be hurt at seeing her card tucked away behind others on the sideboard display. "You're being very quiet, Henry," said his mother, as she deliberated on her problem.

Henry said nothing. He *was* being very quiet. He was not even paying any attention to the television, where a number of policemen wearing flak jackets were leaning over their parked police cars, aiming rifles at the hotel's revolving doors, unaware that the man they sought to capture had already made his escape. But despite the fact that Henry knew that the Count was no longer inside the building, the boy was still concerned on his friend's behalf. He was worried because the Transylvanian noble-man was alone in London and, not for the first time, with every man's hand turned against him. If only there was a way for him to get to London, Henry pondered, then somehow or other he would find the Count. What help he would be able to offer if he should succeed in finding him, was another matter – but at least the Count would know that he was not entirely alone in the world. He would have someone at his side – which, after all, is surely what friendship is all about? But pondering on a trip to London was an entirely different thing to making the visit happen.

"Wouldn't it be great, Mum," began Henry, trying not to sound *too* enthusiastic, "if we could go to London for Christmas."

"London?" murmured Emily Hollins, with a frown.

Emily's frown was not entirely caused by Henry's suggestion. It was partly due to the fact that she was having problems rearranging the Christmas cards on the sideboard. She had moved one card, depicting a cheerful Victorian scene with three Victorian children throwing snowballs at an elderly Victorian gentleman's top hat, towards the left end of the sideboard and moved a second card, a pop-up version of the Bethlehem stable complete with crib, animals and angels, towards the right end of the sideboard. But these tactical manoeu-vrings had not quite made sufficient room to accommodate the silver glitter 'A HAPPY CHRISTMAS' card.

"London?" Emily repeated. "That name doesn't exactly revive many happy memories." She was referring to a previous weekend jaunt in the capital city when Albert, having been prescribed some rather dubious medicine, had been turned into a horrible hairy monster (see *Doctor Jekyll And Mr Hollins*), an experience which Mrs Hollins did not relish going through again.

"But it would be different this time, Mum," said Henry.

"It would need to be," said Emily, giving a distasteful little shiver.

"It *would*," urged Henry. "We could see the Christmas lights in Oxford Street. You and Dad could spend a whole day doing your Chrissie shopping."

"Oh, yes?" sniffed Emily. "And what exactly would you be getting up to while your dad and me were looking round the shops?" Then, before

38

Henry had time to reply, she answered her own question: "All kinds of mischief, I shouldn't wonder – as per usual. No, thanks. I'd rather stop at home and lead a quiet life, if it's all the same to you."

It was true. Emily did have a point. Life in Staplewood, for the Hollinses, was as quiet, orderly and uneventful as any normal family could wish. But, curiously, every time they chose to take themselves off on holiday – if only for a day or two – it seemed that Henry managed to land them in one sort of strange adventure after another. Albert's turning into a horrible, hairy monster had been but one of many weird occurrences that the Hollinses had been forced to suffer. There had, for example, been the occasion when Emily had found herself transported back in history into King Arthur's time – or had that all been in a dream . . .?

"No, London's definitely out of the question this year," said Emily, firmly.

"But, Mum—"

"I mean it, Henry," said his mother, as she tried to concentrate her thoughts on ordinary things. As she spoke, Emily balanced 'A HAPPY CHRISTMAS' on the very front edge of the sideboard where it would be seen to its best advantage should their neighbour chance to pop in. "In any case," continued Emily, as she studied her Christmas card arrangement, "we can't just up-sticks and take ourselves off to London, even if we so desired. There are dozens and dozens of things I have to do, here at home, before Christmas comes. Which reminds me, I must pop down to the shops and get some mincemeat – I'm baking my mince pies this afternoon . . . Oooh, and while I'm in the supermarket, I must remember to stock up on cat food for the holidays." With which, and thus putting an end to all talk of London, she swept out of the room.

The door slammed shut behind Emily, causing a draught which lifted 'A HAPPY CHRISTMAS' from off the edge of the sideboard and sent it fluttering down onto the carpet. Henry had not noticed. He was too busy pondering over his mother's last words. Emily Hollins was muddle-headed at the best of times, and if she was to come back from the supermarket, later that morning, with both mincemeat and cat food, Henry hoped against hope that, when his mother came to fill her mince-pie pastry cases, she would not mistake one product for the other!

Meanwhile, on the TV screen in the corner of the living room, the mob of vampire hunters, unable to track down their quarry, were now pouring out through the hotel's revolving doors.

"Hold your fire, men!" cautioned Police Inspector Andrew Purvis, a red-faced man with a white moustache, as the motley army of chefs, waiters, hotel maids and guests poured out onto the forecourt. The flak-jacketed policemen, surprised by this unexpected turn of events, raised their eyebrows questioningly at one another. "Who's in charge of you lot?" continued the Police Inspector to the assembling crowd.

"I am!" The voice came from Miss Buttershaw who, in the forefront of her troops, was still waving her window pole above her head.

"Then I must ask you to get them off this forecourt and over onto the other side of the road, immediately," said the Police Inspector, officiously. "This hotel is strictly out-of-bounds to all civilians until my men have been inside the building and searched it thoroughly, for vampires, from top to bottom."

"We'll do nothing of the kind!" snapped Amelia Buttershaw. The hotel receptionist, flushed and triumphant after having led her followers up, down, and all around the hotel's many floors, was in no mood to surrender that leadership meekly. "What's more, we *live* here," she added, pushing Purvis backwards with her pole. "We're the ones who took all the risks in there and saw to it that the building is a safe vampire-free area – we're certainly not going to sit out on the sidelines now while you grab all the credit."

As the hotel receptionist and the police inspector glowered at each other with their respective supporters murmuring angrily in the background, the TV camera cut back hastily, to a close-up of Linda Lewington. "Well! The excitement isn't over here by any means!" chirruped the news reporter. "But I'm afraid it's time to return you viewers back to the studio, where the weatherman is waiting to bring you up to date with some rain clouds that are gathering over Spain."

"I've got to find Count Alucard," murmured Henry Hollins as he switched off the television which was now showing a map of central Europe. "I must get to London, that's the important thing."

41

"I must get out of London, that's the most important thing," said the vegetarian vampire to himself, pulling his cloak collar up around his ears. The Count was sitting on a chilly Hyde Park bench, nibbling on a piece of cherry cake which he had just bought in the nearby branch of Marks and Spencer's, throwing crumbs at the several pigeons strutting and pecking around his black-shod feet. "But when? And how?" continued the Count, sucking thoughtfully on a glacé cherry which he had just popped into his mouth, before adding: "And, what's more important, where on earth am I to go?"

The answer to the first two questions "When?" and "How" did not require a great deal of thought. If he waited until nightfall, he would be able to transform himself into his fruit-bat form and thus take wing to wherever fancy might care to take him. But the gift of darkness – beloved by all vampires – was still a long way off. It was still early morning. The urgent sounds of police-car sirens in the distance told him that, in all probability, the search for him was on already. No doubt the general public too had been warned to keep an eye out for him. He could not afford to loiter all through the day in his present state of dress.

Count Alucard looked down and studied his distinctive clothing: the black jacket and the knife-edge creased black trousers; the black patent-leather shiny shoes; the crisp white shirt he always affected. His hand went up to his neck where his long fluttering fingers felt, first, at his black bow tie and then nervously grasped at the gold medallion which hung, as always, around his neck. Lastly, he sombrely examined the black cloak with its distinctive scarlet lining which was draped around his shoulders. It was a stylish manner of dress which had been worn by all of his ancestors before him, but Count Alucard knew that, if the hunt for a vampire was on, he would be noted down immediately by any passer-by as a prime suspect.

He glanced quickly, first one way and then the other. Luckily, for the moment at least the coast was clear. It was a chilly morning and there were few folk as yet out taking the wintry air. All the same, the Count realised that it would not be long before the park would be invaded by the dog walkers, the perambulator pushers and the keep-fit joggers. He would need to find a hiding place, and quickly. . . .

There was a clump of rhododendrons just behind him. Squatting in such surroundings would not be the most dignified way of passing the daylight hours – particularly for a man of the Count's breeding. But as that well-known Transylvanian saying has it: 'The sun never shines down kindly on vampires.'

Tossing the last portion of his cherry cake to the pigeons, the Count rose to his feet and, in several long gangling strides, reached the shelter of the bushes. Just in time! He had barely hidden himself inside the greenery when an old lady, escorted by a waddling Pekinese on a dainty lead and with a pink bow tied on top of its head, appeared around a bend in the path and headed in his direction.

Ducking his head, the vampire Count's eyes chanced to fall on a handbill which had been blown by a gust of wind into the clump of bushes.

It said in large letters on the slip of paper and, underneath this big announcement, in smaller type, were printed the times of the performances. Count Alucard turned the handbill over and surprisingly, spent some time studying the back upon which there was nothing printed. The Count smiled. It was a smile which indicated he was pleased with himself. And why not? The vegetarian vampire Count had just had a good idea – not only that but it had been followed immediately by another! With any luck, put together the two ideas would serve to help him make a speedy escape from London.

"Let go of it!" snarled Police Inspector Purvis as he clung determinedly to the toe end of the slipper.

"I shall do no such thing!" snapped Howard Dobson, the security officer, as he clung equally determinedly to the slipper's heel. "It belongs to me!"

If truth were known, the black velvet item of footwear, with its distinctive gold monogram C. A., was the property of the absent Count Alucard of Transylvania. It was the very same slipper that the Count had lost, the night before, on the hotel staircase. But both the Police Inspector and the security man held different opinions as to the slipper's ownership, which they were now arguing out, in front of the Christmas tree, in the hotel's foyer.

"This slipper is police property," continued Purvis, giving the slipper another quick tug in an attempt to catch Dobson unawares. "It's valuable evidence – it could lead to the capture of a blood-sucking vampire that's been terrorising London."

"If anywhere's been terrorised, it's been this hotel," retorted Dobson sharply, while at the same time keeping up his end of the slipper tug-o'-war. "If anyone's going to catch that vampire it's going to be me – I saw it first!"

They had reached a stalemate. Neither man, it seemed, was willing to give way. Certainly not Purvis. The Police Inspector glanced across at Amelia Buttershaw now back behind the reception desk. He had been forced to back down once that morning – to the forceful arguments of Miss Buttershaw and the threat of her window pole – and allow that lady, and her supporters, back inside the building. But once was more than enough, the Police Inspector had decided. Neither had Howard Dobson any intention of giving way. He had found the slipper in the first place and nothing – and nobody – would make him give it up. While the two men held each other's angry gaze, and kept their grip on the slipper, a Christmas carol, telling of joy and peace and man's goodwill toward his fellow man, came softly over a loudspeaker in the hotel foyer:

> *'God rest ye merry, gentlemen,*
> *Let nothing you dismay,*
> *For Jesus Christ our Saviour*
> *Was born upon this day . . .*

"Permission to speak, sir?"

Police Inspector Purvis turned his eyes to take in the young uniformed police constable who had just entered the hotel. "What is it, Wilkins?" he demanded, irritated by this interruption.

"Sorry to bother you, Inspector, but we've just had a message on the blower," began the young copper, Desmond Wilkins, shuffling uneasily from one booted foot to the other.

"Get on with it, lad!"

"A quantity of vampire's clothing has been discovered in some rhododendrons in Hyde Park."

The Police Inspector's eyebrows shot up at this news and disappeared beneath the peak of his cap. "What sort of vampire's clothing?" he said suspiciously. "How do they *know* it's vampire's clothing?"

"There's a black coat, some black trousers, a posh stiff white shirt, a black bow tie . . ." the young policeman, who was ticking off the items on his fingers, paused and then added significantly: ". . . and a big black cloak with a scarlet lining."

Police Inspector Andrew Purvis whistled softly through his teeth. "That sounds like vampire's clobber right enough, Wilko!" he murmured softly. "This could be just the break we've been waiting for. Come on!"

Without so much as a glance at Dobson, the Police Inspector turned on his heel and strode across the foyer. Taken by surprise, the security officer had almost fallen over backwards when Purvis had suddenly released his grip on the slipper. Recovering his balance, Howard Dobson watched, sadly, as the Police Inspector and his young constable disappeared through the hotel's revolving doors. Dobson sighed and shook his head. He had harboured dreams of being in on the capture of the vampire. He had hoped that he might get his name in the newspapers. Perhaps, even, get interviewed on the telly? Why not? He had been in possession of a 'valuable piece of evidence' – wasn't that what the Police Inspector had called it? But what use was one single slipper now when the police had got their hands on the vampire's entire wardrobe?

Howard Dobson shrugged and tossed the slipper into a wastepaper basket. Squaring his shoulders, he clasped his hands behind his back and strolled off across the foyer about his duties. "You never know, Howard old lad," he muttered in an attempt

47

to cheer himself up, "this could still turn out to be your lucky day – you *might* nab a pickpocket in the Coffee Shop."

Behind the reception desk, Amelia Buttershaw carefully entered the day's date at the top of a new page in the Visitors Book, settled herself on her stool and prepared to welcome any arriving guests. The hotel was getting back to normal.

Things were also getting back to normal on the hotel's forecourt. Most of the police cars and their occupants had already left. Inspector Purvis and Constable Wilkins jumped into the back seat of the one remaining vehicle. "Hyde Park – and quick about it!" snapped the inspector to the driver. "Every criminal makes a mistake sooner or later, Wilkins," he continued, turning to his young assistant, "and, believe me, laddie, this vampire is no exception."

"Why's that, sir? What mistake has he made?"

"Taking off his clothes, of course," replied Purvis, "and leaving them in a clump of rhododendrons. All we have to do now is broadcast to our back-up cars that we're looking for a streaker with pointy teeth – he won't get far without any clothes on."

The police car, its siren blaring, sped off along the main road weaving in and out of the busy morning traffic. Back on the hotel forecourt, all that remained as evidence that a siege had recently taken place, were a couple of empty crisp packets, one of them cheese-and-onion flavour, the other smokey bacon, discarded by a couple of flak-jacketed policemen.

Contrary to Police Inspector Purvis's theory, Count Alucard was not entirely naked. He was still wearing his silk underwear, both of which items, like all of the rest of his clothing, carried the distinctive C. A. monogram. Pinned to his chest was the circus handbill, back to front and bearing the number 13, which the Count himself had added with aid of a felt-tip pen. He had not discarded his gold medallion (a precious family heirloom, handed down by Alucards through the centuries) but had tucked it out of sight, underneath his vest.

Sprinting along the pavement, heading for the outer London suburbs, Count Alucard looked like a stray athlete in a road race or a marathon runner – a rather odd-looking runner, to be sure, on his

spindly legs and with his feet still shod in black silk socks and shiny black patent-leather shoes. But one thing was for certain, if the Count cut an unlikely figure in his guise of English athlete, no passer-by, on seeing the quaint, long-legged, grave-faced figure jog past, would ever guess that he was really looking at a real-life Transylvanian vampire.

It was, of course, all part of the Count's plan to make his escape from London. He was putting into practice the first of the two 'good ideas' which had come to him in the rhododendron bushes.

Count Alucard was panting slightly. He had been running now for quite some time and the route that he had chosen was taking him gradually, but surely, on an uphill course. He was following the road signs which pointed towards Hampstead. Once there, he would bring the second of his 'good ideas' into practice.

While Count Alucard set his plan to get himself out of London into action, Henry Hollins, at home in Staplewood and concerned for the well-being of his vegetarian vampire chum, pondered all morning as to how he might best convince his parents that a pre-Christmas trip to the capital city was exactly what was needed to perk up the family spirits. But when Emily Hollins returned from her visit to the supermarket, she was in no mood to listen to Henry's pleas.

"*No*, Henry!" said Emily, firmly, as she unloaded tins of cat food, jars of mincemeat, a box of Christmas crackers and other seasonal goodies out of her shopping bag and onto the kitchen table. "We cannot possibly go down to London this side of Christmas."

Henry blinked as he watched his mother unintentionally place the jars of mincemeat inside the cupboard where she would normally have put the cat food.

"But, Mum—"

"There are no 'buts' about it, Henry," said Emily, cutting him short, "and if you've got any sense, young man, you'll put any such ideas out of your head before your Dad comes home. He's got goodness-only-knows how many garden gnomes to get packed up and sent off on their merry way before Christmas – he won't take kindly to talk of trips to London—" Emily broke off, a look of horror on her face and a packet of ginger biscuits in her hand, as she heard the sound of a key in the front door lock. "Oh, no! Is that him home for his lunch already?"

It was. There was the sound of the front door slamming then, a moment later, Albert Hollins breezed into the kitchen. He was carrying a wooden crate under one arm. "What ho!" said Albert, cheerily. "What would you pair say to a couple of days in London before Christmas is upon us?"

"London?" said Emily, faintly, as she slipped the packet of ginger biscuits inside the cupboard where she kept her soap powder, furniture polish and other cleaning things.

"Great, Dad!" said Henry Hollins.

"London, Albert?" repeated a rather puzzled

Emily Hollins.

"That's the general idea," said Albert, crossing and placing the wooden crate on the kitchen table.

"I think it's a terrific idea!" said Henry Hollins.,

"But it's Christmas next week," said Emily. "There's a hundred and one things still to be done. And what about the factory? I thought you were rushed off your feet with Christmas orders? And there's the expense to be considered."

"Ah!" said Albert Hollins, importantly. "It isn't going to cost us anything at all. It's an all-expenses paid trip. I'll be travelling down on behalf of the company – on Very Important Business," he added, mysteriously. "As it is so close to Christmas, Mr Winterton suggested that I might take the two of you along as well – as a sort of Christmas treat and also at the company's expense. That's if you'd like to come, of course."

"When do we leave?" asked Henry.

"What about you, Emily?" asked Mr Hollins.

"Of course I'd love to go," said Emily. "You know me, Albert – I'm not one to turn my nose up at a free holiday. But what is it exactly, that is so important that the factory can afford to let you have some days off right in the middle of the Christmas rush?"

"These little chaps," said Albert, proudly, as he lifted the lid off the wooden crate.

# 4

Inside the wooden crate there was a layer of straw
which Albert carefully lifted out, revealing two
shiny garden gnomes lying side by side on a lower
layer of straw. They had painted red jackets, red
pointed caps and blue trousers. They had long
white beards, rosy cheeks, broad smiles and twinkling coal-black eyes. But there the similarity ended,
for while one of the gnomes was leaning on a
shovel, the second gnome was holding a fishing
rod complete with line and dangling plastic fish.
Nestling on their bed of straw, they reminded
Henry of the baby Jesus in his school's Christmas
crib – except, of course, that the baby Jesus was
not wearing a red jacket, red pointed cap or blue
trousers, neither did he carry a shovel or a fishing
rod.

"Ooooh!" exclaimed Emily. "They're posh
ones."

"They're our very first export models,"
explained Albert, proudly. "The first two off the
production line. And they're a special presentation
set from the Chairman and the Board of Directors
at Staplewood Garden Gnomes, as loyal citizens,
to the highest in the land. And I've been dele-

gated to deliver them in person. Don't ask me where." He paused, tapped his forefinger against his nose, and added: "My lips are sealed."

"Can't you give us a clue, Dad?"

"Oh, very well," said Albert, who was unable to keep a secret. "You'd be bound to find out sooner or later, I suppose. The address that they're going to is near The Mall – the first word of its name begins with a 'B' and the second word begins with a 'P'."

"It isn't Battersea Power Station, is it?" asked Emily, after thinking hard.

"No. I said it was two words, not three. And it's a great deal posher than Battersea Power Station, that's another clue for you to think about."

There was another pause and more hard thinking. An idea came to Henry and his eyes slowly opened wide. He blinked twice. "It's not . . ." He paused, gulped, and then began again. "It isn't Buckingham Pal—"

"Ssshhh!" said Albert, pressing a finger to his lips. "I cannot answer that question. I have said more than enough already."

"Wow-eee!" gasped Henry Hollins.

"Well I never!" murmured Emily.


Count Alucard's long, slim forefinger pressed the switch and a light came on in the caravan powered, he guessed, by the big generator he could hear throbbing somewhere outside. The same generator, no doubt, that was lighting up the nearby circus big top where a matinee was in progress at

54

that very moment. The Count could also hear the sound of children's laughter and music coming from the circus's brass band.

"I imagine," the Count said to himself, as he glanced around at his surroundings, "that whoever owns this caravan is probably performing in the circus ring. I shall pen a note before I go, apologising for having trespassed."

Under normal circumstances, the vegetarian vampire would not so much as dreamed of such an intrusion into someone's privacy. But this was no normal circumstance. It was three weeks into December, a chilly, dark and cheerless afternoon, and he was standing in his shoes, socks and under-clothing – the disguise in which he had huffed and puffed his uphill way to Hampstead Heath. The Count shivered, then pulled a face as he glanced down at his inelegant mode of dress. Never mind, he told himself. It had served its purpose. He had passed several road blocks manned by uniformed, armed policemen who had not so much as given him a second glance. What he needed now was a new set of clothing.

Luckily, there was no lack of opportunity on that account in the caravan he had just entered. One whole side of that vehicle was given over to a brass rail on which there hung all manner of men's cur-ious clothing. There were enormous jackets in large-sized checks and in clashing colours. There were lots of pairs of trousers all of which, it seemed, belonged to a gentleman of roly-poly proportions. There were gaudy shirts by the dozen and equally gaudy bow ties in profusion.

Had Count Alucard not been so cold – and therefore so concerned with finding himself some warm clothing, he would have recognised instantly that he had strayed into the caravan of a clown. As it was, the obvious did not occur to him.

"Not *quite* what I was looking for," he murmured, gravely examining a green bowler hat with a yellow band in which was fastened a sweeping peacock's feather.

But as he returned the bowler hat to the shelf from which he had lifted it, the Count's eyes opened wide with delight as he glimpsed exactly what he had been seeking. At one end of the rail, sandwiched between a bright red jacket with pea-green polka dots and a well-worn long fur coat with a huge plastic daisy in its button-hole, was a formal black jacket with matching trousers. Even better, there was a starched white shirt and a black bow tie hanging next to the suit. Count Alucard crowed with delight as he lifted the suit, on its hanger, off the rail and held it up in front of his body. Just about his size!

"I shall see to it that all of these garments are returned to their rightful owner as soon as possible," the Count promised himself as he dressed hastily. "What's more, I shall ensure that the gentleman is suitably rewarded."

Alas though, the man that the suit belonged to must have been a great deal shorter than the Count. His long slim wrists stuck out awkwardly from the jacket's cuffs and there were several inches of his thin legs showing between the trouser ends and his feet. Apart from being too short for him, the suit was much too big around his waist. The jacket, which felt rather bulky, hung on him like a sack, while the trousers flapped around his middle. He was dolefully considering all of these shortcomings when a voice spoke behind his back.

"Someone said there was a light on in this caravan."

Count Alucard spun around and stared, openmouthed and lost for words at the top-hatted, redcoated, chubby-cheeked man with the bristling moustache who had just entered the caravan. "I'm extremely sorry," began the Count. "You see—"

"There's no need to apologise," replied the man cheerfully, stepping forward and doffing his top hat with one hand as he extended the other towards the Count. "I'm only too pleased that you're here at last. Allow me to introduce myself. I'm Sumner Slingsby. In case you hadn't guessed, I own the circus. As you can see," he added, glancing down at his circus costume, "I'm also the ringmaster."

"D-d-d-delighted to make your acquaintance, sir," stammered the Count, putting out his own right hand as he spoke. But, much to his surprise, as he extended his arm, a pair of hideous, writhing, wriggling, greeny snakes shot out of the end of his sleeve and struck the circus owner in the midriff before dropping to the floor where they lay quite still, as though pretending to be dead. "Great heavens!" cried the Count, taking a backward step, partly in horror at what had happened and partly in shock at the realisation that the two fearful reptiles had been hiding inside the jacket he was wearing.

Sumner Slingsby, however, did not seem at all put out by what had happened. Quite the reverse – he threw back his head and roared with laughter.

"I like it! I like it!" guffawed the circus owner and, as he spoke, he stooped and picked up the snakes which, Count Alucard was relieved to discover, were not real creatures after all but "joke" snakes made out of long springs covered in green fabric. "You'd better put them back up your sleeve," continued Mr Slingsby. "You might be needing them again before the afternoon is over."

"No-n-n-no, thank you – you keep them," murmured the Count who, despite the fact that the reptiles were only imitations, was still recovering from the shock of the encounter. But as he stretched out his left hand in a gesture of refusal, another strange thing happened – a long string of pink sausages shot out of his left sleeve and whizzed across the caravan.

"I like that too!" cackled Mr Slingsby, his shoulders heaving with delight.

But Count Alucard could manage nothing more than a nervous smile as he took another backwards step in surprise. It had already occurred to him that the sausages were probably no more real than the reptiles – even so, he was beginning to wonder what kind of suit it was that he was wearing and, what was more to the point, what manner of man would own such a curious garment? It would not be long before he would know the answers to both of those questions.

"I'd better be getting back into the ring," said Mr Slingsby. "The Flying Fantorinis will be finishing their trapeze act soon. As I said, I only popped across to welcome you to the circus."

"Extremely kind of you, I'm sure," murmured the Count, as he ushered the ringmaster towards the door of the caravan. The sooner that Mr Slingsby had gone, Count Alucard decided, the sooner he would be able to get out of the strange suit – which did not fit him anyway – before the jacket did something even more peculiar!

"I don't suppose . . ." said Mr Slingsby, pausing at the door without finishing the sentence.

"Yes?"

"Well – I know that you must be tired after all the travelling you've done – but I was wondering whether you might consider appearing in the circus ring this afternoon?"

"Me?" said the Count, wondering who, exactly, the ring master imagined him to be? And, more important, what he wanted him to do? Whatever it was, the Transylvanian nobleman was incapable of doing it. "Oh, no, I think not – not this afternoon, if it's all the same to you."

"It *is* very nearly Christmas," urged Mr Slingsby, fingering the rim of his top hat. "There *are* hundreds of children sitting out there. They *do* love the clowns – and, after all, you are The Great Gruck – one of the funniest clowns in all the world."

Count Alucard did not reply, but inside his head his thoughts were racing. So that was who the caravan belonged to! The Great Gruck, the famous clown. And he was wearing one of the Great Gruck's suits. Of course! That explained the snakes and the string of pink sausages. And who could tell what other surprises might be lurking still inside the suit? The sooner he was out of it and into some more sensible clothing, the better!

"What about it then?" asked Mr Slingsby, hopefully. The ringmaster had been taking the Count's silence as a sign that he was thinking over the request. "It would make them very happy," he added.

"I'm afraid I couldn't possibly appear this afternoon," said the Count, sadly. "Some other time, I'm sure."

Sumner Slingsby had opened the door of the caravan and, from inside the big top which lay just

60

across the grass, there came the sound of rapturous applause.

"That'll be The Flying Fantorinis doing their mid-air triple somersaults," explained Mr Slingsby. "They'll be taking their final bows in a minute – I really must be getting back into the ring. If you should happen to change your mind about appearing this afternoon . . .?"

Count Alucard gave a sad, apologetic little smile and shook his head. Moments later, after the ringmaster had left, the Transylvanian nobleman sat down at the dressing-table, which was littered with sticks of greasepaint, and gazed, sombrely, into the mirror.

The fact that he did not see his own pale-faced mirror-image gazing sombrely back at him came as no surprise to the Count. Like all vampires, Count Alucard did not possess a reflection. But the fact that he was staring into an empty glass served to make him sadder than ever. The circus ringmaster had mistaken him for a clown! Him! The infamous Count Alucard – the last surviving member of the Transylvanian vampire family! A clown! Why, the very idea was ridiculous! If the children and their parents gathered in the big top were to be informed of his true identity. they would fall over one another in their haste to reach the exits. Ah, he pondered, wistfully, if only he *had* been born into a circus family and not a family of vampires! What a different start in life he would have had! But what was the use of wishing, the Count asked himself as he toyed with a stick of greasepaint? The only course that was open to him now was to put as much distance between the circus and himself and in as short a time as possible. . . . But first, he must scribble that note to The Great Gruck, apologising both for having trespassed and for borrowing the clothing.

But before he could make a move to do so, the Count was horrified to hear, above the music coming from the circus's brass band, the far-off but fast-approaching sound of several police-car sirens. Somehow or other, the police must have picked up his trail. There could be no doubt that they were headed for the circus. Where could he go? Where could he hide? If he tried to run across the open heath he would be spotted instantly. On the other hand, if he stayed where he was, they would track him down in less time than it takes to crack a ringmaster's whip.

Count Alucard again gazed solemnly into the empty mirror. An idea was forming in his mind. An idea so astounding that it almost took his breath away. An idea so preposterous that it did not stand a chance of succeeding – and yet, on the other hand, the desperate situation demanded desperate steps be taken. The Count selected a stick of white greasepaint and, after daubing it in thick broad strokes across his chin and cheeks and forehead, he began to massage it across his skin with the tips of his long thin fingers.

The several police cars screamed to a halt on the area of trodden-down grass between the giant-sized circus tent and its accompanying vehicles. A number of flak-jacketed policemen jumped out, their guns held at the ready. "You lot search all the caravans!" barked Inspector Purvis at the leading group. "The rest of you follow me – we'll search the tent!"

"Who is it you're looking for?" asked a pretty young woman who was wearing a tight-fitting sequinned cap over her golden curls and had a black-lined crimson cloak draped over a glittering sequinned costume. Fay Fantorini, one of the world famous Flying Fantorinis had just come out of the "artists" entrance of the big top and was crossing to her caravan.

"I wouldn't want to alarm you, miss, but it's more than possible that there's a deadly dangerous vampire skulking somewhere in the vicinity," replied the Police Inspector, doffing his hat.

"What makes you think he might be here in the circus?"

"By dint of careful police work, we located most of his clothing in Hyde Park in a clump of rhodo-dendron bushes – following upon which, we've received information from several eye witnesses to the effect that a person answering the monster's description was seen heading in this direction in his underwear."

"In his underwear!" gasped the trapeze artist with a little shiver, drawing her cloak a little closer around her body. "At this time of year? Poor man – he must be freezing!"

"There's no 'poor man' about it, miss," replied the Inspector rather huffily. "He's not a man at all – he's a pointy-toothed monster. Why, he'd have his fangs into your pretty neck as soon as look at you. But don't you worry, miss," he added hastily.

"If he has taken refuge hereabouts, we'll soon have him in custody." Then, turning to the half-dozen flak-jacketed policemen who had gathered just behind him and were staring appreciatively at the trapeze artist, he snapped: "What are you lot gawping at? I thought I told you to search out and apprehend the vampire?"

"Please, sir," began a fresh-faced young constable, raising a hand and blinking nervously, "you told us to follow you – and we can't do that, can we, Inspector? Not while you're standing still."

Several of the other policemen sniggered quietly at this, hiding their mouths behind their hands, while a couple of them laughed out loud openly.

"What's your name, young man?" growled Purvis.

"Police Constable Sefton Hardisty, sir."

"Right then, Hardisty," replied the Inspector. "We'll have a little less of your insubordination in future!" His eyes narrowed as he glowered at the young policeman. Inspector Purvis seemed to remember that he had had cause to question the same constable's devotion to duty earlier that day.

Wasn't it, in fact, the self-same young policeman whom he had noticed on the forecourt, during the hotel siege, tucking into a packet of cheese-and-onion crisps in the shelter of a police car, while all the rest of his squad had been attending to their duties, their guns trained on the hotel's revolving doors? Police Inspector Andrew Purvis made a mental note to keep an even closer eye on Constable Sefton Hardisty in future.

While all of this had been happening, a sad-eyed,

white-faced clown, wearing a white shirt, a white bow tie and an ill-fitting black suit with both the coat sleeves and the trouser legs much too short for his gangly arms and legs, had come out of one of the caravans and was hobbling, in clown's big boots, towards the big top's artists entrance. Police Inspector Purvis had not given the clown so much as a second glance, but Fay Fantorini, a puzzled frown on her pretty face, did not take her eyes off him until he disappeared inside the circus tent.

"Follow me, men!" bellowed the Inspector for a second time. "I'm sure that vampire's somewhere in the circus and he's not going to get away from us this time!"

With the gallant Police Inspector leading the way, the flak-jacketed policemen fairly raced across the grass towards the big top. Fay Fantorini, still deep in thought, moved off in the other direction towards the caravans.

Inside the massive circus tent, the packed audience were paying scant attention to the half-dozen armed policemen who were wandering up and down, searching the tiered rows of seats. There was far too much going on in the circus ring where, under the bright lights, several clowns had recently bounded into view. One clown in particular though, was causing more amusement than all of the others.

If Count Alucard, the Transylvanian vegetarian vampire, in his white-face make-up and with his long thin arms and legs sticking out from his sleeves and trouser-legs, had been harbouring thoughts about failing in his efforts to pass himself off as a circus clown then (as Emily Hollins might very well have put it) "he had another think coming".

From the very first moment that he stepped into the circus ring, under the bright glare of the circus lights and, in doing so, succeeded quite unintentionally in tripping over the clown's big boots which he was wearing, the entire audience – children and grown-ups alike – had taken to him instantly.

Not that the Count was aware of that fact. "Oh, dear!" he murmured to himself as he lay sprawled full-length with his face in the sawdust. "I rather fear that I have made somewhat of a fool of myself!" Struggling to his feet, he put his hand into his trouser pocket in search of a handkerchief with which to wipe the sawdust from his face but, to his surprise, pulled out instead a long, scrawny lifelike plucked chicken fashioned out of rubber.

The audience hooted its delight.

Taken slightly aback at his discovery, the Count took a backwards step in consternation and was shocked still further as a shower of confetti flew upwards out of his top pocket.

The audience roared its appreciation.

As the confetti drifted down and settled on his head and shoulders, Count Alucard gulped with astonishment – an action which, it seemed, set off a tiny motor concealed in the bow tie, causing it to spin round at a furious rate, like a miniature aeroplane propeller.

The audience howled with laughter.

While all of this had been going on, the other clowns had pushed a rickety-looking open car into the centre of the circus ring. One of the clowns

who had a big red nose, a broad red-painted grin, loud-checked baggy trousers and a giant-sized plastic buttercup stuck in his green bowler hat, gestured at the Count with one hand while holding open the car door with his other, inviting him to sit behind the steering wheel.

Count Alucard was only too pleased to take up the kind offer. Still unaware that he had been the big success of the afternoon's performance, the Count's only wish was to put as much distance as was possible between himself and the circus. Out of the corner of his eye, he could see that the policemen were still busy searching the aisles. If he were to make a quick break for it now, they would not even notice that he had gone. The baggy-trousered clown was offering him a golden opportunity. He leaped into the driving seat with the intention of putting his plan into practice. But the car itself had other plans – or so it seemed.

When the Count tugged on the starter, there was an immediate loud explosion accompanied by a cloud of smoke rising out of the bonnet. When he put his foot down on the accelerator, the car set off on a zig-zag course entirely of its own choosing. The more he spun the steering-wheel in one direction, the more the car turned in the opposite path. The diabolical vehicle seemed to have a mind of its own! It travelled round and round the circus ring scattering clowns in every direction and even causing the ringmaster – Mr Slingsby himself – to jump aside.

The audience stamped its feet and cheered.

Finally, having weaved a wayward course for

several circuits of the sawdust ring, the car finally came to a halt of its own accord. There was another loud BANG!, another cloud of smoke, the bonnet flew up while both of the doors and all four wheels dropped off and clattered to the ground. Count Alucard sat quite still for several seconds, stunned by his experience and temporarily deafened by the second of the two explosions. He had suffered, he decided, more than enough! Jumping out of the car, he moved towards the exit – with the baggy-trousered clown now in fast pursuit and carrying, in both hands, a bucket of cold water. Count Alucard, fearing a soaking – for, like all of his vampire forebears, the Count dreaded being drenched with water – ran as fast as he was able. Hampered by his clumsy clown's boots however, he was quickly overtaken by the baggy-trousered clown.

"No! *Please* – no!" wailed the unhappy Alucard, turning to face his pursuer and fearful of what was to come. It was too late. As the Count turned, the baggy-trousered clown, the painted grin spread wide across his face, launched the contents of the bucket straight at the Transylvanian nobleman. Flinching with dread, the Count closed his eyes and cowered. Nothing happened. The expected awful drenching never came. The puzzled Count opened his eyes and realised that the bucket had not held water after all – the confetti that it had contained was swirling all around him as it drifted onto the circus floor.

The audience was rocking with laughter.

Count Alucard's thin shoulders drooped despondently as he turned and trudged out of the circus ring. He had never felt so humiliated in his entire life. He had made an utter fool of himself and felt sure that the laughter, which was ringing in his ears, came out of the mouths of men, women and children who were laughing at his downfall. Miserable, he moved out through the artists entrance canvas awning and shivered in the fading light of the chilly winter's afternoon.

"Just a minute!" The count paused and turned. Mr Slingsby had followed him out of the circus ring. "Well done!" continued the ringmaster. "You were wonderful."

"Wonderful?" echoed the vegetarian vampire, bleakly, scarce able to believe his ears. "*Me?*"

"Of course you were! Why, The Amazing Amorettis have begun their act, juggling with blazing torches – but the audience hasn't stopped laughing at *you*. Just listen to them."

It was true. The gales of laughter could still be heard coming out of the big top. Count Alucard cocked a doubtful ear to the sound. It was not surprising that he found it difficult to believe the circus owner's explanation for the audience's laughter. As a member of the Dracula family he had, after all, spent his entire lifetime being misunderstood and laughed at by the human race. Why, even the local peasants, who lived in the village close by the castle where he had been born and raised, had stormed and burned down that family home, forcing him into exile. Since when, the Count had been hounded, harried and despised all over Europe. It was hard for him, now, to digest the fact that an entire circus audience had warmed to his appearance in the ring.

"Do you mean that they *liked* me?" he asked, tentatively.

"I'll say they *liked* you – they *loved* you!" enthused the ringmaster. "I take it you'll be going on again at tonight's performance?" Then, without waiting for an answer, he added: "We'll be pulling down the big top and moving on tomorrow. Thanks again for appearing at such short notice."

With which, the circus owner turned and moved back into the tent passing en route the dozen or so flak-jacketed policemen led by Inspector Purvis. The policemen barely glanced at the white-faced clown-suited Alucard as they moved towards their parked cars.

"Don't get down-hearted, lads, we'll track him down!" vowed Inspector Purvis, as he squelched his way through a puddle. "He won't get far, believe me – and when we do get hold of the evil blighter, we'll make him sorry he's led us such a dance."

But the Police Inspector's growled threats caused no concern to the Count. To tell the truth, he hadn't even heard them – and this despite the fact that he had been standing no more than a couple of metres from the Police Inspector. The Count, smiling blissfully, was still turning over in his head what the ringmaster had told him: that he had scored a big success in the circus ring. More than that – that the audience had taken him to its heart. *Him*! Count Alucard of Transylvania – a favourite of the general public! That was a turn-up for the books! Perhaps being a clown was not such a bad thing after all? Certainly it would be worth his while to pretend to be The Great Gruck for a day or two more. There was, of course, the vexing question of what he was going to do if the real Great Gruck was to put in an appearance? But he would deal with that situation if and when it chose to arrive. . . .

Across the stretch of grass, the policemen had clambered wearily into their cars – and then most of them had wearily got out again in order to push the vehicles out of the patch of mud in which their back wheels were stuck deep and fast.

Count Alucard, seeing this, chuckled softly to himself as he ambled back towards the caravan. Behind him, the hundreds of different coloured light bulbs strung over and around the big top's canvas roof glowed brightly in the dark of the winter's early evening. The cheerful sound of brass band music – "Oompah!" following upon "Oompah!" – drifted from inside the giant tent, accompanied by a rippled murmur of appreciative "Oohs!" and "Aahs!" and then a burst of applause. The audience was giving its full attention at last to the juggling skills of The Amazing Amorettis. . . .

Yes, Count Alucard promised himself, he would be appearing again in the sawdust ring at that night's performance. And tomorrow, when the circus tent had been taken down, he would be part of the snaking, sprawling convoy of caravans and other vehicles as it set off north – away from London and, more important, away from the clutches of the army of metropolitan policemen who sought to put him behind prison bars.

# 5

"It's no good, Albert," said Emily Hollins, as she gave a little sigh accompanied by a quick shake of her head. "It isn't going to work." Mrs Hollins was sitting on a suitcase on the bed while Albert Hollins pushed and pulled and tugged and did his very best to close it.

It was very nearly bedtime in the Hollins home, on the night before the morning when the family was due to set off for London on the pre-Christmas jaunt. Albert Hollins had decided to pack the night before in order to make an early start. But things were not going as easily as he might have hoped.

"Why not call it a day, Albert?" continued Emily. "Give up for now and try again in the morning."

"I am certainly not giving up, Emily!" panted Albert, as he huffed and puffed and turned quite red in the face. "I refuse to be defeated – I am not going to be beaten by a silly, stupid suitcase!"

But no matter how hard Albert tugged and pushed and pulled, and in spite of Emily sitting on top, the two catches on the suitcase lid stubbornly refused to join up with the two locks on the body of the suitcase – there was only an infuriating centimetre of space between the catches and the locks.

"I think it would be best to pack it in, Albert," advised Emily sensibly. "You're getting all hot and sweaty – and you know what happens when you get hot and sweaty: you finish up losing your rag."

"Excuse me, Dad—"

"Not now, Henry!" snapped Albert, without turning round to look at his son who had just entered the bedroom.

"But, Dad—"

"I said not now, Henry!" continued Mr Hollins testily. "Can't you see I'm busy?"

"He's busy losing his rag," announced Emily, from her precarious position on top of the suitcase, "while I'm perched up here, like patience on the monument."

"I am *not* losing my rag!" retorted Albert, in the sort of voice that suggested he had already mislaid that very article. "But I'll tell you this for nothing – I intend to close this suitcase, if it kills me – presto!" he crowed, triumphantly, as a couple of 'clicks' in unison signified that he had somehow managed to marry catches and locks at long last. "Now – what can I do for you, young man?" he added, turning to face his son.

"You haven't put my things in yet, Dad," said Henry, who was standing by the door of his parents' bedroom, holding a pile of T-shirts, a sweatshirt, a pair of jeans, several pairs of socks and some underwear, with a pair of sneakers resting on top.

"Oh, no!" groaned Albert, turning angrily and flicking open the suitcase catches.

"Whoops-a-daisy!" murmured Emily as the suitcase suddenly sprang open, forced upwards by the mountain of clothing inside and, taken by surprise, she found herself propelled along the suitcase lid and off the bed onto the bedroom floor.

"Back where we started," sighed Albert Hollins, as he gloomily contemplated the open bulging suitcase and wondered how on earth he was ever going to close it again with the extra burden of Henry's things. "It's like trying to put a pint of liquid into a half-pint pot!"

"Never mind," said Emily, cheerfully. "It won't seem half so bad in the light of day – these things never do seem as much of a problem in the morning. Besides, we'll have to pack another case for all our toilet stuff – our Henry's clothes can go in that.

Now, let's do what I said and go to bed and worry about the packing in the morning."

Albert Hollins, in no fit state to argue after all his exertions, feebly nodded his head. Minutes later, the Hollins family had retired for the night.

Resplendent in a pair of paisley-patterned pyjamas, Mr Hollins lay wide awake, while next to him, Emily, who was wearing a pale-blue nightie, had fallen into a dreamless sleep the moment her head had touched the pillow. But Albert was too excited to sleep.

Across the darkened room, tucked safely on top of the wardrobe, Albert could just make out the rectangular shape of the wooden crate containing the two garden gnomes. Albert was wondering if he should turn up in style in a London taxi for his visit to the Palace? Or whether he should savour the experience to the full and stroll slowly to the Palace along The Mall with the wooden crate tucked under his arm? And what would happen, he also wondered, when he presented himself to the Palace sentry? Would he be granted instant access and allowed to walk alone, with measured step, across the courtyard? Or would he be required to wait at the big cast-iron gates while a butler or a footman was sent for to relieve him of the crate? Albert wriggled his toes under the bedclothes in sheer excitement at the prospect of what was in store.

Meanwhile, in the bedroom across the landing, Henry Hollins was also finding sleep difficult to come by. For the second night in succession, Henry was gazing out through the chink in the curtains, pondering on the whereabouts of his friend Count

Alucard. Henry's previous night's wish had been granted. He was going to London. Once there, it would be up to him to seek out his old friend, the Transylvanian nobleman. He realised that it would prove no easy task. Henry Hollins knew London well enough to know that seeking out one person in the vastness of the capital city would be difficult at the best of times – and when that person had gone into hiding, the task could become well nigh impossible. But at least Henry had been granted the opportunity to attempt that impossible feat – and, if luck was on his side. . . . Well, Henry Hollins was a resourceful lad who thought that *nothing* was impossible.

Henry wriggled his toes in excitement under the duvet – like father, like son!

"Ah-whoooOOO!"

Count Alucard stirred in the narrow bunk in the caravan and blinked open a weary eye. Had he, he wondered, really been roused from his slumbers by the howling of a lone wolf, or had he merely dreamed the sound?

The Count certainly had been fast asleep. It had been a busy and eventful day and he had dropped off to sleep as soon as his head had touched the pillow – despite the fact that the pillow was not his to put his head down on. Not that that was an immediate problem. Everyone in the circus, it seemed, had believed him to be the real Great Gruck, the famous clown – and as The Great Gruck himself was not around to contest the fact, the Count was happy to continue with the subterfuge. After all, he told himself, it did no harm to anyone and he seemed to be giving quite a lot of harmless entertainment to a lot of people.

His second appearance in the circus ring, in the role of a clown, had been just as successful as his first. There was no doubt about it, he congratulated himself, he certainly did seem to have the knack for entertaining children. A strange talent to be born with, he mused, for the last surviving member of a Transylvanian family of vampires! The Count chuckled softly to himself, and wriggled his toes beneath the bedclothes as, in his imagination, he relived the pleasures of the day's events in the circus ring.

"Ah-whoooOOO!"

Count Alucard, now suddenly wide awake, sat bolt upright in the bunk and listened hard. Without question, he had heard the call of a single wolf, rising and falling on the still night air. But how could that be, he asked himself? He was not aware of any wolves appearing in the circus – or any other animals for that matter. Slingsby's Celebrated Circus was of the modern kind: there were jugglers, Chinese acrobats, tumblers, trapeze artists, tightrope walkers, a cowboy knife thrower, an illusionist and his female assistant, any number of clowns – but not a single member of the animal world graced Mr Slingsby's circus ring. But if the wolf which the Count had heard baying at the moon did not belong to the circus, then what was it doing on Hampstead Heath . . .?

"Ah-whoooOOO!"

Count Alucard threw the patchwork quilt off the bunk and swung his feet down to the floor. Slipping his feet into The Great Gruck's slippers and shrugging on The Great Gruck's scarlet dressing-gown, the Count eased open the door of the caravan and stepped out into the moonlit night. There was neither sound nor sign of life from any of the tents or from the other caravans. The circus folk were all asleep. Count Alucard stood quite still. The wintry cold from the frozen ground rose up through the frosted grass and struck through the flimsy soles of his slippers. There was a bitter wind too, biting through the thin material of the dressing-gown, chilling the Count to his marrow and causing him to wish that he had not forsaken the comfort of the caravan. He had begun to wonder too, again, whether the wolf's cry had existed only in his imagination – for there was no sound now, save for that of the wind humming through the big top's guy ropes accompanied, intermittently, by the flap-flapping of an unfastened tent door. And then it came again. . . .

"Ah-whoooOOO-OOO!"

Count Alucard set off immediately, with long loping strides, in the direction from where it came. With the moon's assistance, it was not long before he had tracked down the sound. Behind one of the largest circus vehicles – a lorry used for transporting the big top's seating – he came across a small paddock some thirty metres square, fenced with tough steel mesh three metres high, and with a kennel-like building at one end. Inside the paddock, padding nervously around the perimeter and hugging close to the wire mesh, the Count caught sight of an old male wolf.

"Here, wolf!" called the Count. "Here, sir!"

The old wolf, whose nervousness had increased at the Count's approach, was suddenly still at the sound of his voice. Stock-still it sniffed at his scent and peered across at where he stood.

"Come on, wolf! Come here!"

Throughout the centuries, there has always existed a friendship between vampires and wolves. Night-time creatures both, they have frequently sought each other's company. As a boy, in the Transylvanian pine forests, close by the castle where he had been born and raised, Count Alucard had often enjoyed the company of wolves. Spurned by his school fellows because of the name he bore, the young Alucard had found solace with the wolf-pack's cubs. He had plunged waist-deep with them through the winters' snows and gambolled too, head-over-heels, in woodland glades thick with flowers in the summer sunlight.

As if sensing this past kinship, the old wolf padded across to where the Count was standing and, ears pricked and tongue lolling, gazed up at him through the stout wire mesh.

In the pale moonlight, the Count could see that the old wolf's once thick brown-black fur was now sparse in places and heavily streaked with grey and that its lean flanks bore the marks of several past conflicts. There was one long scar too that started above the left eyebrow and ran down the length of its nose, giving the old animal a curiously cross-eyed look.

"My poor friend," said the Count, shaking his head sadly. "Like me, you have known hard times in life as well as good."

The wolf whimpered softly in reply, and nuzzled its nose against the steel mesh in an attempt to rub its cheek against the Count's thigh. But the mesh was too tightly knit for them to make any sort of contact. Sensing that, more than anything else, the old wolf was suffering loneliness, Count Alucard resolved to join the animal in the paddock. Walking along the perimeter, the Count soon arrived at a gate – only to discover that it was securely fastened with a stout padlock. In which circumstance, the Count told himself, if I can't go through then I shall go over.

"Wait, wolf!" he counselled the animal, whose whimperings were increasing by the second. "I shall be in there with you in an instant."

Count Alucard took several backward steps, keeping his eye on the fence and judging the run that he would need to make. Then, having arrived at what he considered to be the required distance, he bounded forward on his long, thin legs, leaped upwards, and grasped the top of the fence with both of his hands. With the old wolf watching him keenly, wagging its tail, the Count succeeded in hauling himself up until he was able to hoist a pyjamad leg over the top of the wire-mesh fence where he rested a moment, regaining his breath.

"And just where do you think you're going?"

Coming out of the shadows, the question totally flummoxed the Count who, with his legs straddled either side of the fence and with his borrowed

dressing-gown flapping in the night air, was forced to turn his head uncomfortably in order to squint down at the newcomer.

"I beg your pardon, miss?" said the Count, politely, gazing down at the pretty, golden-haired young woman who was approaching the fence from out of the darkness.

"You heard me. Come down from there at once!" said Fay Fantorini sharply.

The Count, having already lost one slipper during his exertions, had little option but to obey the trapeze artist's demand. "I do hasten to assure you, miss, I was not intending any harm whatsoever," he said, dropping lightly down onto the grass where he hopped on one foot awkwardly, while he did his best to prevent his bare foot touching the cold ground.

"Then kindly explain to me what you were doing climbing into Carlos's enclosure?"

"Carlos?" Count Alucard raised his eyebrows and his forehead wrinkled into a frown. "Who's Carlos?"

"Carlos the Educated Wolf," said Fay, nodding at the animal behind the fence.

"I only wanted to comfort him,' replied the Count, telling the truth. "I heard him howling in the night and I came out here in order to investigate the sound – I understood that there were no animals in this circus?"

"There aren't. Not any longer. Except for Carlos. All of the others have gone: the elephants, the camels, the seals, the lions and the tigers. Mr Slingsby donated all of them to zoos, or wildlife parks, or animal sanctuaries. And now there's only poor old Carlos left."

"Then why was he not found a home like all of the other animals?"

"Partly because of his age." Fay Fantorini paused and smiled at the old wolf who was peering sadly out at his two visitors, from behind the fence, almost as if he knew that it was him that they were discussing. "He's been a lone wolf now for so many years that it would be cruel to try to put him into a strange pack of wolves."

"It is far more cruel to keep him here like this," countered the Transylvanian nobleman. "Wolves, by their very nature, need to be with other wolves. I feel sure that, given the opportunity, he would very quickly adjust to life with a new wolf-pack."

"And how do you come to know so much about the subject?" snapped Fay Fantorini.

"Because, dear lady—" began the Count and

then broke off. He could not, after all, explain to the trapeze artist that he was well versed in the ways of wolves because he was a Transylvanian vampire Count. Or could he? Certainly it would help enormously if he were to find someone he could put his trust in – for at the moment he was as alone and friendless as the unfortunate creature in the wire-mesh compound. . . .

"And just who are you anyway?" demanded Fay Fantorini, as if reading the Count's thoughts. "And don't try to tell me that you're The Great Gruck – because I happen to know for a certain fact that you're nothing of the kind."

"Oh?" said the Count, uneasily, balancing on one slippered foot, his bare foot still hovering unsteadily in the air above the frozen ground. "Who told you that?"

"Nobody told me. The Great Gruck happens to be a friend of mine – that is to say, he's a good friend of my father's. I've known him ever since I was a little girl."

"It must be good to be born in the circus," murmured the Count, wistfully. "And to grow up among so many friends."

"But I wasn't born in the circus. Neither was The Great Gruck. Before he became a clown, The Great Gruck's name was Bernard Potts. He used to be a milkman in Southend-on-Sea. That was when he knew my father. They went to school together. Bernard Potts left his milk-round and ran away to join the circus. But he and my father have always stayed good friends."

"Then your father isn't one of The Famous

Flying Fantorinis?"

"Of course not! My dad's a dustman. My name isn't really Fay Fantorini – it's Sharon Foster. But I always envied Uncle Bernard's life and so, when I left school, I left home too to join the circus. I sold ice-creams and programmes for a start – but in my spare time I learned acrobatics. I've been a Flying Fantorini now for just over a year."

Count Alucard nodded slowly, digesting every word that Fay Fantorini (alias Sharon Foster) had told him. "I see," he said at last. "The only thing I don't understand is what has happened to the real Great Gruck? And why is everyone – with the exception of your good self – prepared to believe that I am he?"

"Because nobody else in Slingsby's Celebrated Circus has ever seen Bernard Potts. He's spent the last three years in Las Vegas with Thoresby's Three-Ring Circus. He was expected to arrive here yesterday. His caravan came here last week – I promised to look after it. I was *so* looking forward to working in the same circus as Uncle Bernard at last – especially over Christmas. And then you turned up. I knew that you were an impostor from the moment that I set eyes on you."

"And yet, dear lady, you didn't give me away," said the Count, puzzled.

"No."

"And may I make so bold as to enquire *why* you kept the secret to yourself?"

Fay Fantorini frowned and shook her head. "I'm not quite sure," she said at last. "I suppose it must have been because I felt a little sorry for you."

"Sorry? For *me*? But you knew nothing of my circumstances?"

"When that police inspector said that he and his men were looking for someone, I guessed that it had to be you. Then, when he told me that they were trying to capture a pointy-toothed monster – a deadly dangerous vampire – I decided, on the spur of the moment, not to breathe a word to anyone. You didn't *look* like a deadly dangerous vampire."

"Thank you, dear lady, for showing me that kindness. And are you still prepared to trust me?"

"I . . . I'm not too sure . . ." said the trapeze artist, crossing her hands over her chest and rubbing her upper arms against the chill night air. "Looking at you now, out in the moonlight and without your clown's make-up, there does seem something rather strange about you. "You're . . . you're not a deadly dangerous vampire, are you?" she added, hesitantly.

"Dear lady, firstly allow me to assure you that I am in no way deadly, neither am I at all dangerous – as for my being a vampire . . ." Count Alucard paused. Should he continue, he wondered, and confess his true identity to the trapeze artist? She had helped him thus far and, more than anything else in all the world, he was badly in need of someone he could put his faith in . . . *Yes*, he made up his mind. He would unburden himself to this charming young lady – and hang the consequences . . . Finding the courage at last, he lowered his bare foot onto the frozen ground then, standing firm on both of his feet, he spoke up bravely. "As for my being a vampire . . ." he began again.

But he was never to complete the sentence. Before he could add another word, there came the sound of three short, sharp piercing blasts from a police whistle. Dark shapes loomed up out of the shadows of the parked circus vehicles and tents.

"We have the villain surrounded, lads!" cried the voice of Police Inspector Purvis from somewhere in the darkness. "Move in slowly – don't let him get away!"

Count Alucard, aghast, glanced all around him and, with his sharp vampire's eyesight, saw figures advancing slowly upon the wolf's enclosure from all sides.

Police Inspector Purvis and his men had not gone very far when they had driven off in their police cars on the previous afternoon. They had spent some hours unsuccessfully combing the far reaches of the heath. They had thought their endeavours had been rewarded when Police Constable Sefton Hardisty had apprehended a black-suited, white-shirted, bow-tie-wearing, foreign-sounding suspect – but the man had proved to be an Italian waiter on his way to his evening's duties in a nearby restaurant. Reluctantly, they had been forced to let him go. Police Inspector Purvis had given Constable Hardisty a thorough ticking-off – and the search had continued without further incident. But the Police Inspector had continued to harbour a sneaking feeling at the back of his mind that there was a secret yet to be uncovered at the circus.

Knowing that vampires are creatures of the night, Inspector Purvis had waited until the midnight hour before making his move. At which time, believing that all the genuine circus folk would be in their beds and fast asleep, Purvis had stationed his policemen in a wide cordon around the tents and caravans from which position they had advanced slowly on the circus site. Now, having found two people trapped inside his human net, the Police Inspector had no doubts concerning the identity of the trapeze artist's companion.

"Have no fear, young lady!" Purvis yelled at Fay Fantorini. "We'll soon have you out of the evil monster's clutches! He won't dare harm you – not while we're on the job!"

"But I'm *not* in his clutches!" called back the trapeze artist, vexedly. "And he *isn't* going to harm me – or anyone else for that matter!"

But Inspector Purvis gave not a sign that he had heard Fay Fantorini's words – it is doubtful that he had even bothered to listen. Instead, he signalled to his ring of men to advance upon the vampire Count, their weapons held at the ready.

Count Alucard, of course, had one trick left up his sleeve. "Thank you for all of your kindness, dear lady," he murmured quickly to his companion, adding: "Try not to think too harshly of me when you learn the truth of my identity." Then, taking a tight grip with both of his hands on either side of the dressing-gown, he threw his arms out wide. The scarlet garment billowed out behind the Count as the night breeze caught at the scarlet silk. Then, as the advancing ring of policemen came to a sudden halt and let out a concerted gasp of astonishment, the tall, gaunt figure of the Count appeared to shrivel as it turned into his furry-bodied, dark-winged counterpart. Just for a moment, the vegetarian fruit-eating bat hovered at eye-level by the wire-mesh fence and then soared upwards on fast-beating wings towards the twinkling stars.

"Ah-whooOOO!"

Carlos the wolf, the only animal still kept captive in Slingsby's Celebrated Circus, had thrown back his grizzled old head, opened wide his slavering jaws and, for the second time that night, was howling at the moon.

"Ah-whoooOOO!"

Police Inspector Purvis shivered at the unearthly sound and blinked as he stared at the spot where, only a few seconds before, in front of his very eyes, the tall, gaunt man in the dressing-gown had turned into a wing-flapping bat and flown off into the night sky. Walking forward, he stooped and picked up an object which his policeman's keen eyes had spotted on the ground beside the wire-mesh.

"Hey, you laddie! Bung this in the glove compartment," the Inspector barked at Constable Sefton Hardisty, who happened to be the policeman nearest to him. Purvis handed Hardisty the slipper which the Count had dropped during his attempt to clamber over the high fence. "He seems to make a habit of leaving a slipper behind," observed the Inspector half to himself, remembering the gold-monogrammed, black velvet item of footwear which he had tussled over with the hotel security officer on the previous morning. "If you're feeling up to it, miss," he continued, turning to the trapeze artist, "I'd be more than grateful if you'd oblige me with a statement."

Fay Fantorini nodded, without speaking, and moved off with the police officer towards her caravan. On the way, they passed through the ring of policemen which was breaking up and moving off, in twos and threes, towards where they had parked their vehicles.

The old wolf, Carlos, in his enclosure, continued to lament the sudden loss of his new-found friend, Count Alucard, by baying his sadness at the silvery moon:

"Ah-whoooOOO-OOO . . .!"

# 6

"That's a teeny bit morbid, Henry, isn't it?" said Emily Hollins, who had just pulled a face as she had watched her eleven-year-old son reach up and take down a copy of *The Coffin-Maker's Journal*.

"Wow!" gasped Henry as he replaced the journal on the top shelf of the Staplewood Railway Station bookstall. "My mistake, Mum. I thought it was a spooky comic."

Henry had not told the truth. Recognising Count Alucard's favourite reading, he had intended to buy the monthly magazine as a gift which he would give to his friend should he chance to find him. But this was not the time, as Henry well knew, to try to explain to his mother that, while the main purpose of the London trip was for his father to deliver a pair of garden gnomes to Buckingham Palace, his own intention was to scour the streets of the capital city in search of the Transylvanian vegetarian vampire count.

In order to save further questions, Henry chose a less lurid publication from the bookstall's shelves. Emily, meanwhile, had purchased for herself *Jam-Making Monthly* and, for her husband, the current edition of *Gnomes and Gardens*, the fortnightly glossy trade journal of Albert Hollins's chosen profession.

"I hope that you pair realise we've got a train to catch!" said Mr Hollins, popping his head inside the bookstall. Albert had elected to wait outside the bookstall in order to keep an eye on their luggage. "They've just announced our platform on the loudspeaker – if we miss the eight-thirty-two there's not another one until ten-thirty-two."

Moments later, the Hollinses were bustling across the iron footbridge towards their train. Albert, leading the way, was lugging the big suitcase (the one that had caused them so much trouble on the previous night) in one hand while, under his other arm, he kept a tight grip on the precious wooden case containing the garden gnomes. Emily, taking quick short steps in order to keep up with Albert's longer strides, was carrying the smaller suitcase, a bulging handbag and the family umbrella. Henry, bringing up the rear, had been entrusted with a plastic carrier-bag containing all-important items which Emily had forgotten to pack: their toilet things; Albert's spare socks; the hairdryer; Henry's best pyjamas and her own pink comfy fur-lined slippers which went everywhere she went. Henry was also carrying, under his other arm, the several magazines bought at the station bookstall.

Scurrying down the steps towards the waiting train, they could see the guard moving along the platform, slamming carriage doors. A final anxious sprint, in which Emily overtook her husband, saw them safely into a compartment where they settled into their seats as the train moved slowly out of the station.

Then, picking up speed, they moved out into the dark of the December morning where, in the town, the Christmas coloured lights which spanned the high street were twinkling non-stop. Moving on, through the outskirts of the town, they could make out the sprawling complex of one-storey buildings which was the Staplewood Garden Gnomes Company Limited – and Albert gave his workplace a fond wave accompanied by a cheery "Toodle-oo!" as it slipped away behind them in the darkness.

"Do you want to know what I'm looking forward to most of all?" asked Emily, looking over the top of *Jam-Making Monthly* which was open at the centre-page double spread entitled: December's Special Treat – Mouth-watering Mincemeat! "Shall I tell you?"

"No, don't tell us – let me guess!" said Albert. Then, giving Henry a sly wink, he continued: "Sitting in the hotel bar and guzzling a posh cocktail in a fancy glass with a little parasol and a cherry-on-a-cocktail-stick stuck in it!"

"Wrong, clever-clogs," replied Emily, primly. "I'm looking forward to seeing that big Christmas tree in Trafalgar Square – I can't wait!"

With which, she snuggled down comfortably in her seat and gave her full attention to the mincemeat recipe while Albert, sitting opposite Emily, turned over the pages of *Gnomes and Gardens*, lost in the wonderful world of those little people. Henry, sitting in a window seat, was finding it hard to turn his thoughts to his magazine. He was gazing

93

out into the darkness outside the window, ticking off the telegraph poles as they flashed by, counting down the miles that carried him closer – ever closer – to his old friend, Count Alucard.

Or so he thought.

The straggling convoy of gaily painted lorries and trucks and car-drawn cream-and-chromium caravans was stretched out along the motorway that was taking it northwards and away from London. It was half-past eight in the morning but, beyond the orangey glow from the motorway's overhead lighting, it might just as well have been the middle of the night.

Fay Fantorini, at the wheel of the car that was towing The Great Gruck's caravan was almost startled out of her senses as the black bat swooped down from out of the darkness and alighted on the bonnet, taking a tight claw-hold on an arm of the motionless windscreen wiper.

Count Alucard had not had cause to travel far on his bat's wings during the previous night. After having taken flight in order to escape the clutches of Inspector Purvis and his armed policemen, the vegetarian vampire bat had found refuge inside the big top itself. Flying upwards and settling first on the very tip of one of the several giant-sized poles which supported and poked out through the enormous structure, he had crawled in through the gap between the wood and the taut canvas. He had then spent several hours, hanging upside-down and fast asleep, among the guy ropes high up in

94

the roof of the tent. He had been so comfortable, in fact, that he would have slept the whole night through, had he not been awakened, long before dawn, by the shouts of men, the whirr of generators, and the clatter of sledge hammers on metal tubing.

Circus folk are early risers at the best of times, but on moving days, when the big top has to be pulled down and loaded, along with the tiered seating, on the trucks and lorries, they are out of bed and hard at work while the rest of the world is sleeping. These are busy hours during which every member of the circus – man, woman or child – from the biggest star of the sawdust ring down to the humblest programme seller, is expected to muck in and lend a hand.

It was all of this activity, coupled with the sudden glare of the circus arc-lamps, which had disturbed the Count from his slumbers. Before the giant structure had begun to collapse and billow to the ground, he had been forced to crawl out through the roof again, the way he had entered, and seek a safer hiding place. He had settled for a spot high up in the topmost branches of a nearby tree from which vantage-point, and again hanging upside-down, he could observe the big top being dismantled and also give some thought to his own next move.

He could quite easily, of course, in the time that was left to him before the dawn when daylight would demand that he return to human form, have flown away from the circus and put as much distance between himself and London as his wings would grant him. Which would probably have been the wisest course, for there was always the chance that Purvis might return with his policemen. But a little voice inside his head was counselling the Count to discount caution and to stay with the circus.

He did not know why. It could have been caused by the fact that he had so enjoyed his role as a clown – to have human folk applaud and warm to him was a new sensation for the vampire Count. Or it might have had something to do with the kindness that the trapeze artist had shown towards him. Or, perhaps, it could have had something to do with his own concern for the old lone wolf, Carlos, who had seemed as much in need of friendship as he was himself . . . Perhaps it had been an amalgam of all these reasons?

Whatever the cause, when the circus had finally been packed aboard its vehicles, and had set out in slow convoy away from London, the Count had spread his parchment-like wings, fluttered out of the tree, and set off in pursuit.

He had waited until the straggling line of vehicles had moved onto the motorway before swooping down and landing on Fay Fantorini's car. He had, he now realised, waited just a little longer than might have been advisable – for it was at that same precise moment that the first rosy glimmer of dawn began to show itself on the far horizon. At which moment, to his horror and unable to help himself, Count Alucard realised that he was returning to human form.

Fay Fantorini, surprised enough by the bat's

sudden appearance, was startled even more to see the Count himself materialise, perched insecurely on the bonnet of the moving car. He was dressed as he had been attired the previous night: one slipper, pyjamas, and flapping scarlet dressing-gown. It took all of the composure that the trapeze artist could muster to pull out of the line of circus vehicles and safely over onto the motorway's hard shoulder.

"I hope you realise that you very nearly caused me to have an extremely nasty accident!" said Fay Fantorini, after she had jumped out of the car and angrily slammed the door shut behind her.

"A thousand apologies, dear lady," murmured the Count unhappily, scrambling off the car's bonnet onto the hard shoulder where he pulled the dressing-gown tight around his thin frame, as he continued: "I do assure you that it was not my intention to startle you in any way whatsoever – I would not have inconvenienced you for all the grobeks in the world."

"I might believe you," replied the trapeze artist, relenting slightly, "if I had the faintest idea what a grobek was."

"Why – grobeks are the coins we use in the part of the world where I was born," explained the Transylvanian nobleman, hopping up and down on the hard shoulder on his one slippered foot. "There are one hundred grobeks in a zoltar and a hundred zoltars make a—"

"It doesn't matter," broke in Fay Fantorini, noting that the occupants of the vehicles which were driving past were all gazing, open-mouthed, at the curious gangling figure of the Count hopping around in his dressing-gown and pyjamas. "I don't think that this is the time to give me a lesson in foreign currency." She shook her head and smiled – the trapeze artist couldn't help feeling sorry for her companion, and this despite the fact that she had discovered he was capable of turning himself into a bat. "You'd better get inside," she said, nodding at the car, "before those policemen show up again . . ."

Count Alucard needed no second bidding and, a moment later, they were sitting next to each other in the front of the car.

". . . Although why I'm allowing a vampire to sit next to me, I cannot for the life of me imagine!"

"Vampire I may well be, dear lady," replied the Count, sitting proudly upright in his seat, "for I cannot deny the attributes which have been handed down to me by my forbears – but I do hasten to assure you that I am a *vegetarian* vampire and always have been." He paused, ran the tip of his tongue over his pointy teeth, then added: "Speaking of which, I'm feeling rather peckish at this moment – I don't suppose you'd happen to have a nectarine about your person? Or a stray peach, perhaps, or even a juicy plum? I haven't had a bite all morning."

"I'm afraid not." The trapeze artist shook her head as she started up the engine and then eased the car out into the line of passing traffic. The circus convoy had moved on while they had been standing on the hard shoulder and she was going to have to put on some speed in order to catch up with the other vehicles. "I have got some good news for you though," she continued, once they were travelling down the fast lane of the motorway.

"Oh? And what pray would that be exactly?" asked the Count eagerly, for truth to tell he was feeling a little jaded and felt that some "good" news might serve to cheer him up.

"I spoke to my dad this morning on the telephone. And he's been speaking to my Uncle Bernard – you know, The Great Gruck."

"Ah! And what is the news regarding the mysterious absence of that person?"

"Nothing mysterious at all – he's visiting a sick relative in Bournemouth. I'm supposed to tell Mr Slingsby to expect him to join the circus in a couple of days – he'll be here in time for the Christmas Eve performance."

"And when you say that you're 'supposed' to tell Mr Slingsby?" began the Count, giving Fay Fantorini an enquiring sidelong glance. "Does that mean that you are not intending to do so?"

"I haven't told him yet."

"Why not?"

"I was wondering whether you might turn up again. If you want to go on taking his place for a day or two, I wouldn't tell anyone you're not The Great Gruck."

"You'd do that for me still?" replied the Count, gravely. "Even now – since you've discovered the truth about me: that I really am a Transylvanian vampire? Why would you do that?"

Fay Fantorini thought long and hard, her eyes fixed on the motorway, as car and caravan drew closer to the straggling convoy of circus vehicles up ahead. Finally she shrugged. "I don't know why," she said. "Except that I believe you when you say you're not a dangerous vampire. I *trust* you. I would like to help you."

Count Alucard turned his head towards the window. He did not want the trapeze artist to see him blink back a tear. He blew his nose loudly on a handkerchief from out of a packet of paper tissues he had found in the pocket of the dressing-gown. There were some good people in the world, he reminded himself. Henry Hollins for example. In the past, on several occasions, young Henry had proved to be as good a friend as he could ever hope to find. Count Alucard let out a short, sad sigh and wished that he might know of a way to make contact with Henry during his present predicament . . .

"*Do* you want to go on being The Great Gruck?" The trapeze artist's voice broke in on the Transylvanian vampire's thoughts.

Count Alucard pondered over the proposition. It was certainly a good disguise – hiding behind the costume and the greasepaint of the circus clown. And, certainly, he had greatly enjoyed playing the part. On the other hand, if the Police Inspector and his armed policemen should decide to return – and in the hours of daylight – he could not be sure that he could manage to evade them for a second time . . .?

It was while the Count was considering these pros and cons that the car caught up with the line of circus vehicles at last. Last in line in the convoy was a small van which was towing a cage on wheels. Inside the cage, looking equally as downcast as he had done the night before, was old Carlos, the Educated Wolf. But as car and caravan arrived close behind this rear vehicle, the wolf caught sight of his new-found friend of the previous night, Count Alucard, in the front seat of the car. The animal's ears pricked up eagerly, he rose to his full four-footed height, wagged his grey tail, threw back his scarred head and let out a full-throated howl of delight which hung on the wind along the motorway.

"Ah-whooOOO . . .!"

Count Alucard smiled as the sound drifted in through the window. He lifted a long, slim, pale hand and gave a cheery wave at the old wolf. "Taking one thing with another, dear lady," he began, "I do believe that I will take you up on your extremely generous invitation and remain with Mr Slingsby's Celebrated Circus for a day or two."

"Good!" replied Fay Fantorini and, giving the Count a quick smile, she added: "I *am* glad."

"Ah-whoooOOO . . .!"

It was almost as if the old wolf had overheard the conversation and was expressing his own delight at the decision. And, having taken that decision, the Count himself was suddenly more relaxed and settled himself in the passenger seat to take in the passing show of fields and woods and scattered signs of civilisation as he was borne northwards, along the broad motorway.

Henry Hollins wriggled in his intercity seat. He was too excited to take in the passing show of fields and woods and scattered signs of civilisation flashing past outside the window of the speeding train. He was going southwards towards his friend, Count Alucard – or so he mistakenly believed. Across the railway coach table, Emily and Albert Hollins, sitting side-by-side, were also paying scant attention to the outside world. They were both absorbed in the contents of their chosen magazines.

Emily was studying the Readers' Letters page in *Jam-Making Monthly*. An on-going argument took up most of that space in which several readers held differing views as to whether or not marmalade should contain little bits of orange peel. "*My hubby finds all marmalade tasteless if it hasn't got those tangy titbits to nibble on,*" proffered a Mrs Brenda Murchison of Stoke-on-Trent. "*My sister and I are both convinced that shredless marmalade is far more palatable,*" opined a Miss Mavis Primworthy of Bury-St-Edmonds. To Emily, an ardent jam-maker, it was intriguing stuff!

Albert, meanwhile, was immersed in the Letters page in *Gnomes and Gardens*, where argument was currently raging as to whether or not there was a place for lady garden gnomes. "*Over my dead body!*" stated one contributor, tersely, and signed himself: "Disgruntled of Kent". While the Reverend Arthur Cottesloe, of Burton-on-Trent, had written: "*My dear wife, Cynthia, gave me a lady garden gnome for my birthday and we find it has become a talking point for both neighbours and friends.*" To Albert, for whom garden gnomes were both hobby and profession, it made a fascinating read.

"All tickets, please!" said the senior conductor, a beaming black gentleman who had arrived at the table. He wore a gold-braided cap and carried a ticket-punch in one hand.

Albert Hollins put down his magazine, took three tickets out of his pocket and handed them to the senior conductor. "There you go!" he said, good-humouredly.

"These tickets are for London?" said the senior conductor, peering at them through his gold-rimmed spectacles.

"That's where we're going," said Emily enthusiastically, over the top of *Jam-Making Monthly*. "For a few days' break before Christmas – to see the lights in Oxford Street and the Christmas tree in Trafalgar Square."

"*You* may be bound for London, madam," said the senior conductor, turning the tickets over in his hand, "but this train's going in the entirely opposite direction."

"What!" gasped Albert.

"No!" gulped Henry.

"Well, I never!" murmured Emily.

"This is the Edinburgh train," said the senior conductor.

"Edinburgh?" echoed Emily faintly. "But Edinburgh's up in Scotland."

"It is indeed, madam," said the senior conductor with a grin. "Bonnie Scotland – home of the haggis and the kilt."

"But they broadcast that this train was going to London over the loudspeaker on Staplewood Station," said Albert, puzzled. "I heard it most distinctly – the eight-thirty-two from Platform Three."

"Ah – I see now where you good folk have made your mistake," said the senior conductor, removing his gold-braided cap with one hand while he scratched the top of his bald head with the other. "You're not the first by any means – it's very easily done. The eight-thirty-two from Platform Three is the Edinburgh train – this one. What you should have caught was the eight-thirty-three from Platform Two – that's the London one."

"Oh, crumbs," said Henry Hollins, glumly.

*"While Shepherds watched*
*Their flocks by night,*
*All seated on the ground,*
*The Angel of the Lord came down*
*And glory shone—*

The seasonal sound of many voices raised in song was suddenly silenced as Police Inspector Purvis kicked his office door, slamming it shut. The singing was coming from a lecture room across the corridor where the Metropolitan Police Force's Male Voice Choir was rehearsing for its annual Christmas Eve Carol Concert. It was to be a charity performance in aid of all kinds of good causes – but Inspector Purvis had but one good cause on his mind. Namely, the capture and confinement behind bars of the evil vampire monster which had managed to evade him since the early morning of the previous day. Twice he had thought that he had had the monster within his grasp – twice it had succeeded in getting away.

"One thing's for certain," muttered Purvis to himself, as he stood at the window of his upper-storey office, gazing down at the busy London traffic, "it won't get away from me the next time!"

But was there going to be a "next time"? It was a question that the police officer did not like to ask himself. For how could he throw his ring of armed policemen around the evil creature for a third and final time when, truth to tell, he had not the faintest inkling of where to begin to look for his quarry? He had watched, the previous night, with a mixture of horror and tingling fascination, as the vampire had transformed itself from human form to bat shape and then flown off into the night sky. And when you have watched your suspect take wing and head off into the heavens, Purvis put to himself, where do you go for Heaven's sakes, to pick up that same suspect's scent?

In the streets below, fairy lights twinkled in store windows while shoppers thronged the pavements carrying home Christmas trees and gift-wrapped parcels. Christmas was just around the corner, but there was no thought of goodwill towards man in the Police Inspector's heart.

"He's out there somewhere, with his dripping fangs and slobbering jaws," Purvis murmured to himself as he looked down on the seasonal scene, "but *where*? The truth is that I haven't got a single clue – and that's a fact!"

> "—*Thus spake the seraph,*
> *And forthwith,*
> *Appeared a shining throng—*"

Inspector Purvis turned as his office door opened and closed, letting in the sound of the policemen's choir and then shutting it out again.

"Didn't anyone ever tell you to knock, laddie, when you come into a room?" snapped the Inspector.

"Sorry, sir," said Constable Hardisty, setting a cup of coffee in a saucer and a brown-paper package on the desk. "I had both my hands full."

"I hope you remembered to sugar it," growled Purvis then, without waiting for an answer, he picked up one of the two ginger biscuits which were nestling side-by-side on the saucer and dipped it into his coffee. "What's that you've brought in?" he mumbled a moment later through a mouthful of mushy biscuit as he nodded at the package.

"Exhibit 'A', sir."

"Exhibit who?" said Purvis as he picked up and unwrapped the brown-paper package and then stared, without recognition, at the well-worn slipper it contained.

"You remember, sir. It's the one the vampire left behind last night. You asked me to look after it for you."

"A fat lot of use this is," grumbled Purvis, turning the slipper over in his hands. "It wouldn't surprise me if he did it on purpose, just to aggravate us – left a slipper behind at the scene of the crime."

"Has he committed a crime then, sir?" asked Hardisty, for it had suddenly occurred to him that he hadn't been told what it was that the vampire was supposed to be guilty of.

"Flippin' hundreds, I shouldn't wonder, lad," replied the Inspector, gloomily. "He's a vampire, isn't he? Committing crimes is second nature to him. Only we haven't found out about 'em yet. No, and we won't do neither until we've got him safely behind bars and writing out his confession. And I can't envisage that situation ever arising – not if this is all that you can come up with." He paused and curled his lip disdainfully as he contemplated the item of footwear which the vampire had discarded. "One mouldy old slipper! It's not as if it was a pair! We don't know whose it is or where it's been. But I do know where it's going." With which, he drew back his arm and hurled the slipper into his waste-paper bin in the corner of the office.

"Don't do that, sir!" said Constable Hardisty in some alarm, as he retrieved the slipper from out of the odds and ends in the bin. He dusted off the pencil shavings which had somehow managed to become attached to the slipper and then prised off the sticky toffee-wrapper which was stuck on the sole. "I took the liberty of taking it down to the forensic laboratory this morning, sir."

"And a fat lot of good that did too, I'll bet!" scoffed Purvis, although secretly he wished that he had thought of doing exactly that himself. "Er – what did they have to say about it?" he added, trying to sound as if he wasn't really interested.

"Well – they did all sorts of tests on it. Looking for fingerprints and stuff like that."

"And?"

"They didn't find any."

"Huh," sniffed the Inspector. "You don't surprise me. I could have told them that. You don't find fingerprints on a slipper. *Toe*-prints, yes."

"They did find something though."

"Oh?"

"When they examined it carefully through that big magnifying glass they have."

"Really?" The Police Inspector leaned forward eagerly in his chair. "What was that then?"

"Look." Hardisty held the slipper underneath the Inspector's nose and pointed inside the heel. "Whoever it belongs to wrote his name inside it once with a ballpoint pen."

"I can't see anything."

"There." Hardisty pointed with his forefinger. "Most of it is worn away but you can just make out some of the letters."

Purvis screwed up his eyes and peered a little closer. It was true. On the inside of the slipper, up against the heel, he could see some faint ink markings. "I haven't got my reading glasses with me, Hardisty," he said. "What does it say?"

"The first word is 'THE'," replied the constable. "You can see all of that because it's round the side of the slipper where the wearer's heel hasn't rubbed it away. Then there's a 'G-R–'. Then there's a worn bit. Then there's another word with the first letters missing, ending in 'C-K'."

' "THE GR    CK'." Purvis pulled a face. "That's a big help! It could be anything, could that!" he groaned. "THE GRUMPY DUCK –

109

THE GREASY TRUCK – THE GROTTY FROCK. It could be anything at all!"

"I think it's somebody's name, Inspector," said Hardisty quietly. "Not only that, sir – I think I know whose name it is."

"Go on."

"Take a look at this," said Hardisty, opening a folded handbill which he had taken from his pocket. "I picked it up at the box office last night to give to my old mum – she's rather partial to the circus." He held the handbill out so that the Inspector could read it. It was a publicity handout for Slingsby's Celebrated Circus, similar in size to the one that Count Alucard had come across in the clump of bushes in Hyde Park. Except that this one listed all the famous attractions which could be seen in the circus. Constable Hardisty ran his forefinger down the list:

**THE FLYING FANTORINIS**
(Dare-Devil Trapeze Artists)
**THE AMAZING AMORETTIS**
(Unique Juggling Skills)
**THE INCREDIBLE IVANOVS**
(Artistry on the High-Wire)
**THE HILARIOUS HUGOTS**
(King & Queen of the Uni-Cycle)
**THE GREAT GRUCK**
(World-Famous Clown)

Constable Sefton Hardisty's forefinger came to a stop as it arrived at the clown's name, halfway down the handbill. "There, sir!" he said. "There's a name that starts with 'G-R' and ends with 'C-K'."

"You're not suggesting, are you, Hardisty, that The Great Gruck is really a blood-drinking monster?" replied Inspector Purvis, sourly. "My missus would make my life a misery if I put a clown in clink over Christmas."

"I'm not saying he's the vampire, no, sir," said Hardisty. "But we do know for a fact, sir, that the vampire's been borrowing this clown's slippers. We've seen him wearing them. So they must know one another. It's the only clue we've got, Inspector" urged the constable. "I can't see that we've got anything to lose by following it up and having a word with The Great Gruck."

"More easily said than done, laddie," replied Purvis with a sigh. "I happen to know for a fact that Slingsby's Celebrated Circus packed its bags and moved on this morning. It could be anywhere by now. We don't know where it's headed and, what's more, we've no way of finding out."

"But we *do* know where it's going, sir. It says so on that handbill that you're holding."

"What a stroke of luck!" murmured Purvis softly as he looked down at the piece of paper which he held in his hand. In big letters, across the top of the handbill, it stated the name of the town where the circus was due to appear over Christmas. "I've never heard of the place," added Purvis with a frown.

"I have, Inspector," proffered the constable. "It's up north, sir. Just off the motorway. If we get our skates on we could be there this afternoon."

"Right then!" When Police Inspector Andrew Purvis made up his mind about anything, he became a man of instant action. "Get the lads together and tell them to assemble in the car park in ten minutes' time," he added, handing Hardisty back his handbill.

"I'm afraid I can't do that, sir."

"Oh? Why not?"

"They're all sitting in the canteen, sir. Cook's dishing up his special Chrissy lunch today. Roast turkey, sage-and-onion stuffing; little chipolata sausages; roast spuds and two veg, with Chrissy pudding and custard to follow. I'm on my way down there myself. We've even had a whip-round for a box of Chrissy crackers. There'd be murders on, sir, if I tried to get them into the car park before they've finished eating."

Police Inspector Purvis drew in his breath, sharply, in vexation. "Oh, all right," he said at last. "But I want them on parade, armed to the teeth, in their flak-jackets and ready to move off, as soon as they've had that Chrissy pud – no hanging about for coffee and after-dinner mints or any of that malarkey."

"Righty-ho, Inspector," said Hardisty, heading towards the door. "Thy will be done."

"Just a minute!" yelled Purvis as Hardisty put his hand on the door handle. "What did you say that town was called? The one where the circus is headed for?"

"Staplewood, sir. I looked it up this morning in a guide book in the library. It's a little market town. Charles Dickens is supposed to have stayed there once. But it's best known now for its garden gnome factory – it's supposed to be the biggest one in Europe." With which, he opened the door into the corridor and, once again, the sound of carol singing drifted into the office from the nearby lecture room:

> "—sailing by, sailing by!
> I saw three ships go sailing by,
> On Christmas Day in the—"

And was gone again, as quickly as it had arrived, as the door swung shut on the departing Hardisty who was off in pursuit of his Christmas lunch.

Purvis got to his feet and glanced, admiringly, at the framed photograph of himself, hanging on his office wall, which had been taken on the proud day when he had won the police station's Annual Snooker Competition. "Staplewood here we come, Andrew!" he observed to his shirt-sleeved photograph self.

"Staplewood, d'y'say? Oh aye, I know the place fine." Jamie McPherson kept his eyes on the motorway as he steered his vehicle southwards. "It'll be nae bother at all to take a wee detour and drop you safely off on y'r doorstep."

Emily, Albert and Henry Hollins, sitting in a row alongside Mr McPherson in the huge cab of his container lorry, exchanged relieved and happy glances with each other. Their luck, it seemed, had taken a turn for the better. And about time too!

They had got off the train at Newcastle – which had been the first and only stop the intercity express was to make before its arrival in Edinburgh. They had planned to catch the next train which would take them back the way they had come and then on to London. Alas though, as they were quick to discover, things were not quite that simple. Their problems did not end at Newcastle – they had only just begun.

To begin with, on presenting themselves at the ticket office, they had learned that there would not be another London-bound train for well over an hour. Worse still – much worse! – when Albert had put his hand inside his jacket for money to buy new tickets, it was only to discover to his horror that his pocket was empty. With a sinking heart he had remembered that, in his haste to leave the house that morning, he had left both his money-clip and his credit-card case behind. The maddening thing about it was that he knew exactly where they were. They were sitting, side-by-side, on the sideboard in the living-room – slap bang in front of the Three Wise Men Christmas card which had been sent to the Hollinses by Uncle Sumner. Albert had put both money-clip and credit-card case in that prominent position in order not to forget them.

"Perhaps if we went and saw the station master and explained our predicament, he might take pity on us?" Emily had ventured as the three of them had stood forlornly on the station concourse, dwarfed by the station's tall Christmas tree, while more fortunate mortals with money in their purses or their pockets and in possession of tickets, had scurried past them in both directions. "Perhaps he might let us come to some arrangement?" Emily had added lamely.

"What sort of an arrangement?" Albert had grumpily replied. "A sort of travel-now-pay-later arrangement? I very much doubt it. Besides, we'd still arrive in London without a penny-piece in our pockets."

"I've got five pounds and forty-five pence, Dad," Henry had said, having rifled his money-box before leaving home that morning in order to finance his search for the Count.

"Thanks very much, son," his father had replied with a sigh, shifting the wooden case containing the garden gnomes from one arm to another as he spoke, not daring to put it down with the rest of the luggage. "But five pounds forty-five pence won't get us very far in London."

"We could get some coffee and a coke for Henry now," Emily had put in, glancing over at the station buffet. Several hours had passed since they had breakfasted and Mrs Hollins was beginning to feel quite peckish. "I'm not asking you to *give* me the money, Henry," she added hastily, "just to lend it. There might even be enough to run to chocolate chip cookies all round."

"We haven't got time for cups of coffee, Emily," Albert had said sternly, "let alone chocolate chip cookies."

"But that man behind the counter in the ticket office told us that there wouldn't be a train for well over an hour."

"Exactly so," Albert had replied, picking up the bigger of the two suitcases with his free hand and gesturing with his head at both his wife and son to follow him as he set off, briskly, towards the station exit. "We haven't got time to hang about – we're going to hitchike home."

"Hitchhike?" Emily had echoed, horrified, picking up the smaller suitcase and breaking into a trot in order to keep up with Albert's long strides.

"*Home*!" Henry had echoed, equally dismayed. The chances of him finding his friend, Count Alucard, appeared to be diminishing by the minute.

"To pick up the money and the credit cards," Albert had explained. "We're going to have to go back to square one and start all over again."

Which was how the Hollinses came to be sharing the cab of the juggernaut with its bearded Scottish driver, Jamie McPherson. Henry's five pounds and forty-five pence, in company with the loose change they had managed to put together from out of the several compartments of Emily's purse and Albert's trouser pockets, had proved sufficient funding to provide their bus fares to the motorway junction just outside Newcastle. It was there that the friendly Scot, who was taking his juggernaut's load of haggis across the channel, had taken pity on the Hollinses, having spotted them by the roadside.

They were headed southwards now en route for Staplewood. It was a prospect which Henry was none too pleased about. He had hoped, by now, to have been searching the streets of London for the absent Translyvanian Count. But had Henry Hollins been aware of the adventures which were waiting for him in the normally quiet backwater which was his own home town, he would have realised that he was headed for as much excitement as any eleven-year-old could hope to expect.

"You great soft silly pudding, Hardisty!" snapped Police Inspector Purvis, sternly. "I hope you realise that you're a positive disgrace to the police force!"

"Me, sir?" said Constable Hardisty, blinking and wrinkling his forehead.

Sefton Hardisty was genuinely puzzled. He had – or at least he *thought* he had – done everything that the Inspector had asked of him. He had assembled the squad of policemen, in their flak-jackets and armed with their automatic rifles, out in the car park and ready to move off in the vehicles which were drawn up behind them. Not only that, but he had managed it with several minutes to spare.

It had been no easy task to prise the policemen out of the canteen after they had finished their Christmas dinners. Generous portions of good food had left them feeling a little lazy. Some of them had wanted to hang around at the table in the hope of second helpings of the cook's delicious Christmas-pudding-and-custard, while others had dawdled over the contents of the Christmas crackers, swapping the jokes and posing the riddles. But Constable Hardisty had wheedled, cajoled and even threatened and, at long last, had managed to persuade them where their duty lay. And now, standing at attention in front of the entire squad, when he had expected praise from his superior officer, he was getting criticism.

"Yes, you laddie!" growled the Inspector. "Do you usually present yourself for inspection with one of those things on your head?"

From the ranks of the men behind him, Hardisty could hear several muffled sniggers. With a sinking feeling, he gingerly raised a hand towards his head. His fingertips touched flimsy paper and his worst fears were instantly realised. He was still wearing the hideous yellow paper hat from out of his Christmas cracker.

"Blimey O'Riley!" mumbled the constable under his breath. The stifled sniggers coming from the policemen at his back were growing louder by the second. That was what annoyed him most of all. They were supposed to be his chums and yet they had allowed him to turn up on parade wearing a Christmas cracker paper hat. They were *enjoying* his humiliation. "They're more like little kids than coppers," Hardisty thought to himself.

"And you can just cut out the giggling, Constable Grimshaw!" bellowed the Inspector. "You're hardly in a position to find fault with anyone – look at yourself, lad."

Hardisty swivelled his head just far enough to catch a glimpse of Constable Arnold Grimshaw, a chubby policeman wearing steel-rimmed spectacles. Grimshaw, who had managed to down second helpings of everything, had forgotten to take off the paper napkin decorated with little Santa Clauses, which he had tucked into the front of his shirt collar to stop himself from spilling gravy

119

down his tie.

"Don't do that with it, you moron!" roared Purvis as Grimshaw, realising what he was still wearing, had plucked out the offending napkin, screwed it up and tossed it aside. "Pick it up and put it in the litter bin. This is a parade ground, not a rubbish tip."

As the chubby policeman bounded across the parade ground in pursuit of the paper napkin which was bowling along in a breeze, Constable Hardisty allowed himself a little smile. "Serve him right too!" he observed to himself.

"Pay attention the rest of you!" snapped Inspector Purvis. "It might be very nearly Christmas, but there's a deadly blood-drinking vampire at large in England – in case it had slipped your memories. And we're going to nab the evil creature. When I give the command 'Move', I want to see you all inside your vehicles, double-quick, and ready to set off. Follow my car out of the car park – we'll pick up Constable Grimshaw on the way . . . Yes, what is it now, lad?" he said, with a sigh, as Constable Hardisty shyly lifted a forefinger and wiggled it in the air.

"Will it be all right if I go back to the canteen first, Inspector, and fetch my uniform cap?"

"No, it will *not* be all right, Hardisty," growled Inspector Purvis. "As a matter of fact, it would be all wrong!"

"But, sir—" began the constable, knowing that he presented a ridiculous figure in his Christmas cracker paper hat.

"You heard me, laddie! You came on parade in

that clown's costume – as far as I'm concerned, you can go on wearing it – all day long."

"But, sir—"

"Shut up!" Then, without giving the young policeman time to say another word, Inspector Purvis turned his gaze upon the rest of his squad and bellowed: "MOVE!"

Seconds later, with Hardisty at the wheel of the leading car, still wearing his Christmas cracker paper hat, and with the grim-faced Inspector Purvis sitting beside him, the convoy of police cars streamed out of the police-station car park. The line of vehicles, containing the squad of heavily-armed vampire hunters, turned right through the main gates and headed towards the motorway which would lead them northwards. They paused only momentarily in order to pick up Constable Grimshaw who was standing at attention next to the litter bin where he had deposited his napkin.


"There, boy!" said Count Alucard, tossing the beefburger inside its bun through the bars of Carlos's cage. "Eat! Enjoy!"

With an agility which belied its years, the old wolf sprang across and caught the tasty morsel between its fangs before it touched the floor. Then, throwing back its battle-scarred head, swallowed the burger in a single gulp.

"Ah-whoo-grrr . . ."

It was not a howl, this time, that came out of the old wolf's jaws – it was a long, low growl. It was a growl grunted partly in appreciation of the speedily departed hamburger and, partly, in recognition of the kindness of the provider of that tasty morsel. Count Alucard put his hand through the bars and ruffled the greying patch of fur on top of the animal's head.

"Ah-grrr-whooo . . ."

"He seems to like you."

Count Alucard turned in surprise to discover that his friend, Fay Fantorini, had approached quietly and was standing at his shoulder. "Old Carlos and I have much in common, dear lady," he began. "We were born within a wolf's howl of each other. In our youth we roamed the same pine forests that stretched beyond the Castle Alucard in the far-off country where I was born."

"Did you really?" Fay Fantorini did not think to question how the Count had come by the information regarding Carlos's original habitat. After all, when you have seen a person shrivel into a bat in front of your very eyes, and then take off on parchment-like wings into the night sky, you can believe that person capable of many things . . . "The same country where a hundred grobeks add up to a zoltar?" she said instead, remembering their conversation earlier that morning.

"The very same, dear lady."

"What is that country called?"

"Transylvania."

Fay Fantorini made no reply. There was not a great deal to be said. She had read sufficient books and seen sufficient late-night movies on television to know that Transylvania was the home of all vampires. And, while she was prepared to trust completely the tall, gaunt, sad-faced man in the ill-fitting borrowed black suit, the very mention of the country that he came from was sufficient to send little shivers darting up and down her spine.

Count Alucard was also silent. He too was thinking of Transylvania. But the Count's thoughts were entirely pleasant ones. His mind had turned to memories of Transylvanian Christmases long past: of blazing log fires in huge stone fireplaces; of candle-lit Christmas trees glimpsed through peasants' windows; of the massive oak carved table that positively groaned with cakes and fruits and

sweetmeats on Christmas Eve in the vaulted dining-hall at Alucard Castle; of old Yakov, the manservant, who had been happy to pull him on his sledge through the snow-carpeted forest, without complaint for hour after hour. Dear good, kind Yakov . . . He often wondered what had become of the old retainer . . .

Lost in their separate thoughts, the Transylvanian vampire and the pretty trapeze artist were barely aware of the sounds of activity going on not far from where they stood. Earlier that afternoon, the two of them had helped the other circus folk erect the big top. They had tugged and heaved on the long, thick ropes which had hauled the massive poles up into position. They had taken their place, too, in the long line of bodies which had hauled and pulled and man-handled the canvas roof up to dizzy heights.

Now, with the vast canvas covering of the big top in place, the small army of tent-men were preparing the interior for the early evening's performance: building the scaffolding framework which would hold the tiered ranks of seating; sledge-hammering home the iron pegs which would hold the tough canvas walls fast. In less than a couple of hours, the enormous tent would need to be ready to accommodate the Staplewood towns-people and children, but there was still much work that needed to be done.

"I must be getting back," said Fay Fantorini, breaking into Count Alucard's thoughts. "I promised to help Mr Slingsby in the ring. You will be ready, won't you, for the first performance?"

"But of course, dear lady!" The Count gave the trapeze artist a quick, reassuring smile. "I wouldn't miss tonight's performance for the world. I'm looking forward to it enormously."

But the Count was not being entirely truthful. In his heart of hearts, he was experiencing some misgivings. Some sort of vampire's sixth sense was giving warning that the evening would hold more in store for him than the fun and frolics of the sawdust ring with the other clowns. As he watched Fay Fantorini turn and move off towards the big top, the smile faded from his face. "But whatever fate and ill-fortune thrust upon me tonight, my friend," he continued, turning back to the old wolf inside its travelling cage, "be sure that you shall not go forgotten."

As if in answer, Carlos, now squatting, paws extended, thrust out his neck, lifted his head, opened wide his mouth and, this time, let out a familiar long baying howl.

"Ah-WhoooOOO . . .!"

"My goodness, Mrs Hollins," said Jamie McPherson, glancing round the living-room of 42, Nicholas Nickleby Close, in admiration. "You've certainly done well for Christmas cards!"

"Yes – we thought so too," said Emily, proudly. "This one's our favourite," she continued, pointing at the Cheeky-Robin-Sitting-On-The-Christmas-Pudding card which 'the nice couple they had met on holiday at Scarcombe' had sent them. "How do you take your tea, Mr McPherson?" Emily added, crossing to the tea-trolley she had wheeled into the room.

"With a wee drop of milk and just one teaspoonful of sugar – if it's nae trouble."

"No trouble at all, Mr McPherson," said Albert Hollins, who was standing in his favourite spot with his back to the fireplace – even though there was no fire – thumbing through the evening paper which he had collected from the doormat and which Emily had forgotten to cancel at the newsagent's. "A cup of tea and a couple of ginger nuts are the very least that we can offer after all the kindness you have shown by bringing us to our very doorstep. What do you say, Henry?"

But Henry, hunched on the sofa, looking as miserable as he felt, could manage no more than the bleakest of smiles in reply to his father's question.

"Cheer up, Henry!" said his mother, handing their guest his cup of tea with two ginger nuts balanced on the saucer. "We are still going to London – it's just that we won't have quite so long to spend there as we originally planned."

But Emily's words were of little cheer to her downcast son. In fact, she had put her finger on the very reason *why* he was downcast. The shorter the time they spent in London, it seemed to Henry, the smaller were his chances of finding his friend, the Transylvanian vegetarian vampire Count.

"I think I know how the wee lad feels, Mrs Hollins," said Mr McPherson, dipping a ginger nut into his tea. "London's a fine place for a lad to be when it's close to Christmas, ye ken – what with the lights and the shops and all. And I suppose y'r boy's been looking forward to the trip for weeks?"

"Oh, but he hasn't, Mr McPherson," said Emily. "As a matter of fact, we didn't even know about the trip until yesterday. We're going down to London because—" She broke off, wondering if she had already said too much, her eyes fixed on the all-important packing case which Albert had refused to let out of his sight and had placed, for safekeeping, on top of the television.

"Harrumph!" Albert Hollins cleared his throat importantly. "I'm sure it's safe to tell Mr McPherson why we're London bound, Emily. I think we know him well enough by now to know that we can trust him to keep our little secret."

"My lips are sealed, Mr Hollins," replied Jamie McPherson, leaning forward in his seat, partly out of eagerness to hear what the Hollinses had to say, and partly in order not to drop any soggy ginger nut crumbs in the armchair he was sitting on.

"Go on then, Albert," said Emily, proudly. "You tell him."

Albert Hollins cleared his throat again, then: "You have probably heard of the Staplewood Garden Gnomes Company Ltd?" he said.

"Who hasn't?" replied Jamie McPherson with a nod. "Not only have I heard of them, but I've got one of the wee bearded fellows sitting at the side of the fish pond in my own back garden. Mrs McPherson is awful fond of it."

"I work at Staplewood Garden Gnomes," said Albert Hollins, modestly.

"Aye, well . . ." replied Mr McPherson, dipping

his second ginger nut in his tea. "I had you marked down as a man of some importance the minute I clapped eyes on you."

"That packing case on top of the telly, Mr McPherson, contains a pair of garden gnomes destined for great things."

"Ye dinna say?" said the Scot, leaning even further forward with his half-eaten ginger nut poised between cup and mouth.

"They're bound for Buckingham Palace, Mr McPherson, and I have been honoured with the task of personally delivering them."

"The Lord moves in mysterious ways, Mr Hollins, as the Reverend McAllister was moved to observe in the pulpit last week."

"I beg your pardon?" said Albert, puzzled by the remark.

"Look out there," said the Scotsman pointing at the living-room window which overlooked the front garden and the Close beyond. "Tell me what you see."

Albert, more puzzled than ever, did as Mr McPherson had told him. He frowned, shook his head and shrugged. "I can't see anything at all," he said. "Your juggernaut is blocking the view."

It was true. The enormous motor vehicle, which Mr McPherson had parked outside the Hollins's home, not only blocked the view from the window, it also took up every centimetre of parking space in Nicholas Nickleby Close.

"It's my vehicle I'm asking you tae take a look at, Mr Hollins," replied Jamie with a throaty chuckle. "Tell me what you see on the side?"

128

"McWHINNEY'S WORLD FAMOUS HAGGIS," said Albert, reading out the wording which was painted in big flowing letters across the juggernaut's side.

"And what's written under that?"

Albert Hollins crossed over to the window for a closer look. "There's a painted crest," he said. "With a lion and a unicorn on either side of a crown."

"Aye – and tell me what it says underneath the crest?"

"By Royal Appointment," said Albert, screwing up his eyes in order to read the small gold lettering.

"Your garden gnomes are not the only goods that are on their way to Buckingham Palace, Mr Hollins," said Mr McPherson. "Before I take the cross-channel Ferry, I'm due to deliver half-a-dozen family size haggis to that very same prestigious address, ma'sel'."

"*You're* going to Buckingham Palace too?" gasped Emily.

"Ah'm a frequent visitor, Mrs Hollins," replied the juggernaut driver. "Oh, aye – I ken well how proud y'r hubby feels at being entrusted wi' the honour of delivering the first two garden gnomes to the Palace." Jamie McPherson paused, smiled at Albert, and then continued: "I ken fine the time that I delivered my first brace of haggis – I've been going in and out through those gates for years now but, truth to tell, I still get a tingle up the spine when I drive past those sentries."

"Well!" gasped Emily, a little overawed at being in the same room at the same time as two men of such importance – particularly in the knowledge that one of them was her husband. "What a coincidence," she added.

"Birds of a feather flock together, Mrs Hollins," observed Jamie McPherson, cheerfully, then turning to Albert he continued: "And considering that we have so much in common, Mr Hollins, how would you and your family feel about travelling with me for the rest of the journey?"

"All the way to London?" said Albert, raising his eyebrows in appreciation of this generous offer.

"It's a very kind thought, Mr McPherson," said Emily, "but I don't think that we would want to put you to so much trouble."

"Nay trouble at all. You've seen for yourselves that there's more than enough room for us all up inside that cab. And, to tell you the honest truth, I much prefer a bit o' company. *You'd* be doing *me* a favour. It's a lonely life at the wheel of one o' they great things." Mr McPherson nodded at the giant vehicle which loomed large outside the living-room window. "If I might be so bold as to make one suggestion though."

"Please do," said Albert. "Feel free."

"There's nae sense in driving down to London late this afternoon – they don't take deliveries at the Palace when it gets tae tea-time an' they're tucking into their crumpets an' their triangular cucumber sarnies an' aw' that. We'd be far better making an early start tomorrow morning. I'll find a bed-and-breakfast boarding house, here in Stapleford, and I'll call round for you at the crack of dawn—"

130

"You'll do nothing of the kind." broke in Emily. "I wouldn't dream of letting you! I'll make up a bed in the spare bedroom, Mr McPherson. And you can be sure that I shall see you get a nice bacon-and-egg breakfast before we set off in the morning too."

"That's awfu' kind of you, Mrs Hollins."

"Not at all. If you're driving us all the way to London, it's the very least that we can do. One good turn deserves another, Mr McPherson."

"If not two good turns," added Albert Hollins, nodding at the evening newspaper which he was holding open. "I see from this advertisement that Slingsby's Celebrated Circus has come to town. Why don't I see if I can get some tickets for the early evening performance for all four of us? And you shall be our guest."

"That would be nice," said Emily.

Albert had two reasons for making this suggestion. Firstly, he felt, like Emily, that he would like to show his appreciation in return for Mr McPherson's generosity in offering them the hospitality of his driving cab. Secondly though, he had noticed how despondent Henry seemed – which was not like the boy at all. And particularly so close to Christmas. Henry was, by nature, a chatty and a carefree lad. Mr Hollins hoped that by proposing the visit to the circus, he might succeed in cheering up his son. Alas though, Henry gave no sign that an evening at the circus would do anything to raise his spirits. In fact, it almost seemed as if he hadn't even heard the proposition.

Sitting with his elbows on his knees, his chin

131

buried in his hands, Henry Hollins looked the very picture of gloom, hunched on the edge of the sofa. But if he could only have known that the circus visit would result in uniting him with his long-lost chum, Count Alucard, Henry would have jumped up and down with delight on that very same article of furniture.

# 8

A glance into his rear-view mirror reassured Constable Sefton Hardisty that the several police cars, all identical to the one that he was driving, were still strung out in line behind him in the middle lane of the motorway. With their sirens blaring and their blue lights flashing, the police convoy presented an impressive sight, causing other cars and lorries to move over into the slow lane in order to allow them right of way. It all served to make Sefton Hardisty feel proud to be a policeman. It made him feel that all those long years of arduous training had not been in vain. At the same time though, and also in his rear-view mirror, the young constable caught a glimpse of his own appearance and that served to make him feel rather foolish.

"Can't I take it off now, please, sir?" begged Hardisty of the Inspector who was sitting beside him. "I feel like a proper Charlie – driving along the motorway in a Christmas cracker paper hat."

"Certainly not!" snapped Purvis. "Serve you jolly well right. You'll take it off when I decide, laddie, not before. In any case, you *are* a proper Charlie. If I'd have been daft enough to go on parade in a silly hat when I was a young copper,

Hardisty, I'd have never heard the last of it – I'd still have been pounding the beat. I didn't get promoted to Inspector, you know, by going around in a Christmas cracker paper hat."

The young constable let out a sigh and then felt it best to change the subject. "Supposing this clown, The Great Gruck, does turn out to be the vampire, sir?"

"There's no doubt about it, Hardisty," replied Purvis, who had already convinced himself of that fact – mainly because he was aware of the trouble in which he would find himself for bringing an entire convoy of policemen up the motorway if his suspicions were to prove incorrect. "The Great Gruck *is* the blood-sucking vampire all right, Hardisty, you mark my words. All the evidence points to that fact."

"Okey-dokey, sir. Let's say you're right and that he is this evil creature – what do we do when we confront him this time?"

"Why – nab him, of course, you ninny! Slap the handcuffs on him double-quick. Sling him in a cell and throw away the key." Police Inspector Purvis smiled a little self-satisfied smile, paused, then added pompously: "So that the citizens of this green and pleasant land of ours – men, women and kids alike – can enjoy a Happy and a Peaceful Christmas without going round worrying whether they're going to get a couple of pointy fangs stuck deep into their necks."

"But supposing he turns back into a vampire-bat, sir," persisted Hardisty, "like he did the last time, and flies off into the sky again? Won't we have had another wasted journey?"

"What time do you make it, constable?"

Sefton Hardisty glanced at the wristwatch which his mother had given to him many Christmases before. Mickey Mouse's hands were stretched out horizontally in opposite directions. "It's a quarter to four, sir. Why do you ask?"

"Good. With any luck we'll be in Stapleford by half-past four, or thereabouts – in which case, he won't be able to turn himself into a vampire-bat, will he, lad?"

"Won't he, sir?"

"Not if it's still afternoon, you thickhead! Vampires can only turn themselves into bats when it is night-time. Everyone knows that."

"It gets dark very early, sir, at this time of year."

"Dark afternoons are hardly the same thing as the dead of night," snapped the Inspector. "Believe me, Hardisty, I've seen every late-night horror movie that's ever been shown on the telly – and I've yet to see one where Dracula goes round terrorising peasant folk at tea-time," Inspector Purvis paused, smiled a little secretive smile, and then added: "Besides, even if he should turn back into a bat – I've got another trick left up my sleeve."

"What's that, sir?"

"Look up there," said Purvis jabbing a stubby thumb towards the clouding sky.

Constable Hardisty took his eyes off the motorway ahead and glanced upwards through the side window. Up above the convoy, swaying in the December wind, two helicopters were scudding in tandem, keeping up with the police cars.

"They're both equipped with searchlights and automatic weapons," said Purvis, grimly.

"Brilliant, sir!" said Hardisty, impressed. "However did you manage to get them?"

"I got on the blower to New Scotland Yard while you and your chums were busy stuffing your faces with Christmas pudding," said Purvis sourly. "What's more – they've even got radar. Those two beauties can home in on any moving object, large or small, from miles away. The vampire hasn't been born yet, Hardisty, that can combat that kind of modern-day technology. Believe me, Hardisty," Purvis allowed himself a little smirk, "that vampire hasn't got a chance."

"Brilliant, sir," said Hardisty again.

But inside his heart of hearts, when he considered the possibility of the small black bat caught in the searchlights' crossbeam, wheeling, twisting, frightened and temporarily blinded by that glaring light, Sefton Hardisty could not help but feel a tinge of pity for the nocturnal creature. Besides, he asked himself, weren't bats supposed to be an endangered species? And, if so, would such a rule apply to vampire bats . . .? Not that the young constable would have dreamed of posing such a contentious question to his commanding officer . . .

"Get your skates on, Hardisty!" growled Inspector Purvis, his voice breaking in on the constable's thoughts.

Obeying the order, Constable Hardisty increased his foot pressure on the accelerator and eased the vehicle into the fast lane of the motorway. The convoy of police cars followed him, snake-like. Overhead, the two helicopters hovered over the line of vehicles as it headed purposefully northwards and towards the Staplewood turn-off.

The old wolf lay on the floor of his cage, ears pricked, tongue lolling and panting softly. Carlos was deep in thought and, because thinking was something he rarely attempted, it was not a process that came to him easily. The animal was struggling to remember things that he had not attempted to bring out of the box of memories inside his head for many years.

It was all because of the minutes he had spent with his new-found friend, the Transylvanian Count. There had been something strangely comforting, the old wolf had instantly realised, about the presence of the newcomer to the circus.

The animal's sight was not as keen as it had once been, but its sense of smell was largely unimpaired. And it was the newcomer's scent that had turned the old wolf's mind to thoughts of days long past. Not the scent given off by the clothes the Count was wearing, for that was the self-same smell that Carlos was wont to encounter from all of the circus folk who approached his cage or compound. No, it was the newcomer's *man*-smell that was different. A man-smell is an odour indistinguishable to man himself, but instantly recognisable by every keen-nosed animal in the wild. The man-smell which this newcomer gave off stirred memories in Carlos' mind which took him back to his wolf-cub days. Memories of pine-scents in wide-reaching forests. Other memories too – of the crisp, clear scent of early morning air lying still over vast miles of untrodden snow. And the scent of snowdrop shoots pushing up through the forest floor when winter's snow has melted into the very first beginnings of spring . . .

Carlos had never considered himself at all unhappy during his long years with the circus. What could he have to complain about when he had shelter, was well-fed, and constantly provided with clean straw? Nevertheless, it did occur to him that there was something missing from his life. What Carlos wanted – although because he was a wolf he could not quite comprehend the thought – was his own space.

Sinking his nose between his outstretched front

paws, he began to whimper softly to himself. Lost in thought, Carlos was unaware of the throb of helicopter engines overhead.

"OOMPAH-PAH,
 OOMPAH-PAH,
 OOMPAH-PAH-PAH—"

The circus bandsmen, dressed in their bright red tunics, navy-blue trousers with broad red stripes down the sides and gold-braided caps, were playing a rousing tune as the early-evening chattering audience took their seats.

"Ah'm awfi' glad you invited me to join you, Mr Hollins," said Jamie McPherson, settling himself into one of the four ringside seats which his host had been lucky enough to acquire.

"I'm only glad that you were able to come, Mr McPherson," said Albert Hollins, passing a programme to Emily who was sitting between himself and Mr McPherson, with Henry, still downcast, on Emily's other side.

"Oooh!" said Emily, giving a little shiver as she craned her neck to peer upwards towards the big top's roof where two tiny platforms, with rope ladders dangling down from them, and positioned breathtakingly far apart, marked the points from where the world famous trapeze artists, The Flying Fantorinis, would hurl themselves out into thin air. "You wouldn't catch me going up there – not if they paid me," continued Emily, adding: "What about you, Henry?"

"Not for a million pounds, Mum," said Henry Hollins, with a quick shake of his head.

"Not for all the garden gnomes in Staplewood," joked Emily Hollins.

Henry Hollins managed a grin at last. He had decided that as there was absolutely nothing he could do, for the time being at least, about the problems that were tormenting him, he would put them out of his mind and concentrate instead on enjoying the circus. After all, he told himself, his vegetarian vampire friend was a hundred miles away and more . . .

The truth of the matter was, of course, that at the self-same moment, Count Alucard was no more than a dozen metres or so away from Henry Hollins' ringside seat. Dressed in his Great Gruck's badly fitting dinner-suit costume and wearing his white-face make-up, the Count was standing in the shadows, in the artists' entrance, also waiting for the show to start. Although he was not due to make his own clown's entrance in the ring for some minutes to come, the Count was newcomer enough to circus life to enjoy and absorb everything that went on.

Count Alucard who, like Henry Hollins, was eager to forget his problems, gave a little wriggle of anticipation and folded his thin arms across his chest as the tent lights dimmed and, simultaneously, a battery of floodlights suddenly lit up the circus ring.

The early evening performance of Slingsby's Celebrated Circus was about to commence – more important, it was to prove to be an entertainment that the entire audience would have cause to remember for the rest of their lives.

"Ah-whooOOO . . .!"

"Ooh-er!" gulped Constable Sefton Hardisty, nervously clutching at Inspector Purvis's uniform sleeve. "What was that, sir?" The hairs had risen up along the back of the young policeman's neck, rustling against the bottom of his Christmas cracker paper hat.

"Get off, Hardisty," growled the Inspector, brushing aside the constable's hand. "Whatever it is, it's outside – not in here with us."

It was almost dark and the two men were standing close together in The Great Gruck's caravan. Finding the vehicle unattended and with the door unlocked, Purvis had detailed the rest of his squad to remain outside while he and Hardisty examined the interior for clues. But once inside, with the door shut and in the near dark, they were both quick to realise that there was something slightly spooky about the caravan – perhaps it was the shadowy rail full of clown's clothing where, it seemed to them, a vampire could be lurking behind each and every garment.

Inspector Purvis tugged a policeman's torch out of his pocket and switched it on. The beam of light restored a little of his confidence. "Pull yourself together, Hardisty!" he snapped at the young constable whose teeth were chattering noisily. "You're supposed to be a copper, not a cry-baby."

"Sh-sh-sh-shouldn't we have asked per-per-per-

141

mission, sir?" stammered the constable. "B-b-b-before we came inside? Oughtn't we to have a search warrant?"

"We're hot on the trail of a deadly dangerous vampire, Hardisty!" snarled Purvis. "You can't afford to say 'Please' and 'Thank you' and 'By your leave', lad, when you're dealing with an evil pointy-fanged monster."

"But that's exactly what I mean, sir. Supposing that the vampire comes back while we're in here, in the dark . . ." And Constable Hardisty paused to cast another fearful glance towards the darkest part of the caravan where the sinister row of clown's clothing hung ominously still and silent. "S–s–supposing he's in here *now*, sir, hiding, watching us—"

"Shut up!" said Purvis nervously. His torch beam fell on an article underneath the clown's make-up table. "Pick that up and bring it over here."

Constable Hardisty stooped, picked up the item and held it under the light of the torch. There was no doubt about it! It was the matching slipper to the one the vampire had discarded before taking wing the previous night.

"It's even got the same ballpoint pen marks inside the heel," said the Inspector. "And these aren't quite so worn away as those other ones – you can read the name quite clearly: THE GREAT GRUCK."

The two men stood in silence and in gathering darkness as they gazed at the slipper in the torch's beam.

"Ah-whooOOOooo . . .!"

This second wolf howl, like the first, had drifted into the caravan through a part-opened window. They could also hear the sound of a drum roll, rising and falling on the night air and coming from the big top as one of the circus performers paused, dramatically, before attempting some nigh impossible feat.

"There's no doubt about it, Hardisty," said Purvis, flicking off the torch. "This is all the proof we need."

Outside, some twenty or so shadowy figures, silhouetted against the bright lights from the big top some several hundred metres away, turned respectfully as Inspector Purvis appeared in the caravan's open doorway with Constable Hardisty peering eagerly over his shoulder.

"We've got him this time, lads!" announced Purvis. "He's inside the circus tent right this minute." He paused as an excited murmur of anticipation ran through the ranks. "We'll move in quietly, surround the big top then, when I give the word – we pounce!"

With a wave of one hand, the Inspector signalled to the policemen to follow him as he set off across the grass towards the warm glow of light and the sound of music coming from the circus. On their way, crossing the moonlit car park, they were grateful for the shadow afforded them by the massive juggernaut in which Jamie McPherson and the Hollins family had driven from Nicholas Nickleby Close to the circus site in Peggotty Park. Arriving at the back of the circus tent, Inspector Purvis came to a halt and again held up a hand.

"Spread out now, lads," he whispered. "Form a circle around the tent and I want two of you positioned at every entrance. Quick as you can now – and quietly – *move!*"

"*Ow-er!* That hurt!" exclaimed a voice a moment later.

"Who said that?" hissed the Inspector.

"Sorry, sir. It was me, sir." The familiar voice came from a shadowy figure which was scrambling to its feet.

"Trust you, Hardisty!" growled Purvis.

"I think I must have tripped over a guy-rope," explained the young constable. "I banged my shin on a tent-peg – I haven't half hurt it!" he added, ruefully, rubbing at that area through his policeman's thick trousers.

"Shut up, laddie."

"Very good, sir."

After which, there was nothing but silence, save for the throbbing of the helicopters' engines in the dark sky overhead, as Inspector Purvis stared at the luminous hands of his wrist-watch. He waited until the second hand had ticked twice around the face then, judging that he had given his men sufficient time to get themselves into position, he hissed: "We're going in now – pass it on!"

"We're going in now – pass it on!" echoed Hardisty to the constable positioned, some distance away, on his other side.

"We're going in now – pass it on . . ."

In this manner, the order was delivered all around the outside of the big top. Then, when word came back to the Police Inspector, he raised

144

his right hand yet again and, with a cry of "Forward!" led his force into the circus.

The operation to apprehend the vampire was about to enter its final phase.

## 9

"Oompah-Pah-Pah-Pah,
  Oompah-Oompah,
  Pah-pah-pah—"

Inside the big top, with the band playing softly
in the background, Emily Hollins, Albert Hollins,
Henry Hollins and Jamie McPherson, in company
with the rest of the audience, held their breaths
and strained their necks as they gazed up into the
air, open-mouthed, at where The Incredible
Ivanovs, the world famous tightrope walkers, were
performing their act. With similarly bated breath
and still standing in the shadow of the artists'
entrance, Count Alucard was also watching the
daredevil feats of the Ivanovs in fascinated awe and
amazement.

"—Oompah, Oompah, Oompah, Oompah,
  Oompah, Oompah, Oompah, Oompah—"

They were the sounds of muted saxophones that
caught exactly the excitement of the moment as
the handsome Ivan Ivanov, in his skin-tight sequinned suit, hovering perilously high-up over the

circus ring, carefully slid first one foot and then the other along the taut high wire. In front of him, he was pushing his equally handsome twin-brother, Ilya, in a wheelbarrow, while their sister, the incredibly beautiful Olga Ivanov, was perched on Ivan's shoulders, gripping the small of his back with her feet and holding in her hands and across her chest, the long balancing pole upon which the trio's safety depended.

Suddenly, the excitement was over. The Ivanovs had safely crossed the wire and had arrived at the other side. The three tightrope walkers sprang lightly onto the platform and waved their hands in unison, acknowledging the rapturous applause while the band "Oompahed!" triumphantly.

Then, as several circus hands ran into the ring from one side and began to dismantle the tightrope's steel supports, the gang of clowns, with the white-faced Count Alucard in his ill-fitting black suit and gangling on his long legs in their midst, burst on from another direction. At that same moment too, Fay, Freddo and Filippo Fantorini – The Famous Flying Fantorinis – somersaulted into the arena in order to take up their positions, high up on the tiny platforms, when the clowns were ready to take their bows. For it was the golden rule in Slingsby's Celebrated Circus that there should never be so much as a moment's pause in the continuous entertainment.

"Stop the show!" bellowed an important sounding voice from somewhere at the back of the tiered seating. Before the audience had time to turn their heads to see where the voice came from, Inspector

Purvis, who had ideas of his own regarding the continuity of the entertainment, holding his police identity card above his head for all to see, was striding down towards the ring. "I am Police Inspector Purvis!" he went on, addressing the circus staff, the clowns and the trapeze artists who had frozen where they stood at his command. "I must ask you all to stay exactly where you are until I give the word."

While Purvis had been speaking, his constables had taken up their positions at every exit and were now moving down the aisles, in pairs, cutting off every avenue of escape. One of these policemen, some members of the audience were surprised to note, was wearing a Christmas cracker paper hat.

"There is nothing to fear, ladies and gentlemen," continued Purvis, now addressing the audience. "As soon as we have apprehended the dangerous villain we have come here to collect, the circus will be allowed to proceed." Then, turning back to the puzzled occupants of the ring, he glowered fiercely at the bunch of clowns. "All right! Come clean!" he thundered. "I want the truth! Which one of you lot is The Great Gruck?"

The clowns exchanged nervous glances and shuffled uneasily on their big-booted feet, but not one of them breathed so much as a word. For while circus folk as a breed are recognised to be a close-knit band, there is a particular bond of loyalty between the clowns. True to this code, the clowns that worked at Slingsby's Celebrated Circus would not have dreamed of tittle-tattling on the recent arrival to their company – certainly without knowing first the full circumstances of the case.

Count Alucard however, did not stay long enough to put the loyalty of his new-found friends to the test. As the Police Inspector strode into the ring, the vegetarian vampire Count turned tail and fled.

"Stop that clown!" yelled Purvis, giving chase himself.

With policemen advancing on the arena from all directions, the Count was left with no alternative but to run round and round the ring with Purvis in hot pursuit.

The other clowns did everything they could to aid the Count's escape while, at the same time, doing everything that was possible to hinder Purvis. One of them stuck out his clown-size boot and tripped up the Inspector. Another clown squeezed a rubber bulb in his trouser pocket which was attached by a tube to a plastic flower in his button-hole, sending a shower of water into the Police Inspector's face as he ran past. A third clown – the baggy-trousered fellow with the giant-sized plastic buttercup in his bowler hat, launched the entire confetti contents of his bucket over Purvis.

The audience, puzzled at first at the goings-on, were now beginning to think that all this was part and parcel of their evening's entertainment. They hooted with laughter at the sight of the Inspector tripping up over the clown's big boots. They shrieked with joy when the spray of water struck him in the face. They hooted with delight as the shower of confetti was flung all over him. The entire audience, that is to say, with the exception of one small boy sitting in a ringside seat.

At first, Henry Hollins had failed to recognise his chum, Count Alucard, in the ill-fitting clown's borrowed suit and the white-faced make-up. Now, with the arrival of the police, he had at last seen something strangely familiar about the tall, thin, gangly-legged figure careering round and round the circus ring in ever decreasing circles, pursued by an irate Police Inspector.

"Count Alucard!" breathed Henry Hollins softly, suddenly sitting upright in his seat.

For the Count himself, with the laughter of the audience ringing in his ears, it was time for desperate measures. Despite the help from his fellow clowns, he knew that the Inspector was beginning to catch up with him. Not only that, but several of the policemen were now clambering into the ring. Then, out of the corner of his eye, he saw a means of possible escape. Dangling from somewhere high up in the roof of the massive tent was one of the two white rope-ladders that led up to the tiny platforms from which the Famous Fantorinis launched themselves out on their trapezes and flew off into the air in all kinds of daring double and triple somersaults. For a split second and no longer, Count Alucard hesitated.

When he was in his bat-form, the vegetarian vampire had no fear whatsoever of heights. On the contrary, given the opportunity and on the darkest of starless nights, it would afford him the utmost pleasure to go scudding high among the tips of the trees in the tallest of forests – or soaring in and out of the TV masts and electric cables over any skyscraper city. And why shouldn't he indeed? He had every faith in his fine, strong bat's wings and had his unerring radar-like sixth sense to guide him. In his human form however, the Count was a nervous person who was terrified of heights. Under normal circumstances, he could not so much as climb up onto the third rung of a step-ladder without feeling queasy. He could not step up onto a chair to change a light bulb without feeling a nervous tremble in his knees.

For this reason then, there was that split-second of hesitation before he grasped with both hands at the dangling rope-ladder. Then, sensing the hot breath of Inspector Purvis on the back of his neck, Count Alucard set off up the ladder, hand over hand, and taking it two rungs at a time on his long legs, without pause and without so much as a backward glance.

"Don't stand there watching, Hardisty!" growled Purvis at his constable assistant who had arrived on the scene. "Get after him, lad!"

"Me, sir?" quavered the young copper, who had no great head for heights himself.

'Yes, sir. You, sir," mimicked Purvis. "And get a move on too! You're not afraid of climbing up a rope-ladder, are you?" he added sneeringly, although if the truth be known, he was none too brave himself when it came to rope-ladders.

By now, a number of policemen had gathered at the foot of the ladder as the vegetarian vampire continued his ascent towards the trapeze artists' tiny platform which, looking smaller than ever, was situated high up near the big top's canvas roof.

Constable Hardisty gulped twice and then he, too, lifted his hands above his head and took a firm grip on one of the rope-ladder's shiny steel rungs. The audience's laughter had stilled as, wondering what was going to happen next, they gazed up at the man they took to be The Great Gruck who seemed to be moving more slowly now as he climbed higher and higher still. The audience, the circus folk and the policemen alike, all strained their necks as they watched Constable Sefton Hardisty, his Christmas cracker paper hat set firmly on his head, pursuing the clown up the ladder.

"Good on you, Sefton!" called out one of his fellow policemen, urging the young copper on.

"Go get him, Sefton!" yelled another.

"Let's hear it for the clown!" cried out a member of the audience, overhearing the policemen's shouts and believing still that what was happening was all part and parcel of the entertainment.

"Yes!" echoed a little old lady who was gripping the handle of her handbag with both hands excitedly. "Go on, you Great Gruck!"

Upon which, other members of the audience took up the shout on the clown's behalf and a ragged cheer of encouragement went up from the tiered seating.

"He's not a clown! He's a deadly dangerous vampire!" howled Police Inspector Purvis. "You'd all be sorry if he stuck his pointy fangs into your necks." But his angry words were drowned in the cheering.

"Good luck, Count!" murmured Henry Hollins, softly to himself, as he watched his Transylvanian friend climb higher and ever higher.

Spurred on by the burst of cheering from below, Count Alucard had moved more quickly and had almost arrived at the tiny platform. What he was going to do though, once he was on it, he had not the faintest of ideas. No matter, he told himself. At least he had made some attempt at escape. He had done his best, and no Transylvanian nobleman can do more that that . . .

Rope-ladders, for those that are not used to them, are difficult and tiring things to master. The Count was all but exhausted as he hauled himself, at last, onto the trapeze artists' platform. There was only just sufficient room for him to sit, his long legs dangling over the edge. As he paused to regain his breath, he could hear the puffs and pants of the man who was pursuing him. Count Alucard held tight onto the ladder and tried to summon up sufficient nerve to peer over the platform's edge.

"Don't look down!"

The warning voice, which the vampire Count had instantly recognized, had seem to come from out of thin air. Peering across the vast floodlit space of the upper big top, Count Alucard saw Fay Fantorini standing, a world away it seemed to him, on a tiny platform identical to the one on which he was perched.

The young lady trapeze artist, who had set off for her high-placed platform before Purvis had interrupted the proceedings, looked resplendent in her sequinned body-hugging costume. Apparently uncaring of the fact that she was standing, precariously, high above the circus ring, she was poised,

gracefully, with one hand on her own rope-ladder, her other hand casually holding the trapeze which she had unhooked from a rope above her head.

"Stand up!" counselled Fay from across the arena, adding: "Don't be afraid."

"But I *am* afraid, dear lady!" called the Count, nervously, sitting as far back as was possible on his platform, his hands beginning to shake.

"Trust me!" the trapeze artist called back across the wide expanse of space. "Stand up – *please*!"

Partly in the courage that he took from these words and partly driven by the knowledge that his pursuer was only a few metres away on the rope-ladder, Count Alucard rose slowly to his feet. His knees trembled, his hands were shaking as he clutched tightly on to the ladder for support. Heed-

ing the trapeze artist's previous words, he did not look down but kept his eyes fixed firmly on the upper part of the massive tent and its canvas shrouded roof.

"Take hold of the trapeze!" called Fay Fantorini.

Glancing up, the Count saw a trapeze identical to the one that Fay Fantorini was holding just above his head. Bravely, he loosed a hand from the rope-ladder's support and raised it to unhook the shiny metal bar which swung free to dangle in front of his face.

"Take hold of it with both your hands!" called Fay Fantorini.

Ah! How much easier said than done! It was a command that the vegetarian vampire Count found himself unable to obey. He could not, no matter how hard he tried, summon up sufficient courage to loose his other hand's grip on the rope-ladder's support. To do so would result in him standing upright on the tiny platform with both hands clutching on the bar of the swinging trapeze. And *why*? What *for*? Even if he did succeed in summoning up the nerve required, he asked himself, what would he gain by swinging over to the other side? There were as many policemen swarming at the foot of Fay Fantorini's ladder, as there were at the foot of his own. On the other hand, of course, there was no policeman yet with the courage to climb up the opposite rope-ladder. If he *could* just call upon some inner reserve of courage, at least there would be temporary safety on the other side . . .

"You *must*!" urged Fay Fantorini. "There's no other way!"

Out of the corner of his eye, Count Alucard could see the blue uniform of a policeman wearing a Christmas cracker paper hat on his head and about to arrive on the platform.

"Good lad, Hardisty!" roared Inspector Purvis from the ring below. "Go get him! Fetch him! Bring the wicked blighter down!"

It was these words that wrought a sudden change in the Count. He would *not* allow himself to be captured easily. Not while there was an ounce of Transylvanian blood left in his body. He was not, by nature, a brave person. But there were times, he told himself, when a man should strive to attempt the impossible – if only for his own peace of mind.

One by one, he released his fingers' grip on the rope-ladder's support. A moment later, to his own astonishment, he found himself standing upright, unsupported and unafraid on the platform, his hands gripping the free-swinging trapeze in front of his face.

"When I call 'Jump!' you must jump!" cried Fay Fantorini, across the yawning space that separated them.

"Whatever you say, dear lady!" replied the Count, in a voice so calm that it did not sound like it came from him.

"*Jump!*"

Having already taken the decision to jump, the act itself was surprisingly easy. Count Alucard leaped from his tiny platform at the very same moment that Fay Fantorini launched herself, on her own trapeze, from the other side.

"OOOOOoooooohh!" a great sigh of wonder rose up from the entire audience.

High above the circus ring, as the two trapezes swung to their limits and then back again, Fay Fantorini secured her legs around her trapeze bar and was hanging upside down, arms extended, hands open to catch the Count.

"*Let go!*" she cried.

On this command, Count Alucard released his hold on the trapeze bar.

What happened next was a moment that the vegetarian Count would relive, over and over again, in his mind's eye, for the rest of his life. During these reflections, he would be forced to admit to himself that it was his own fault entirely that he did not end up in Fay Fantorini's safe hands. He was, it is true, no more than a split-second too late in releasing his grip on the trapeze – but it was a split-second that made the difference between success and failure.

Fay Fantorini swung past empty-handed while Count Alucard, to his absolute horror, felt himself falling through thin air and hurtling towards the ground.

A split-second later, on widespread bat's wings, the Count was soaring upwards towards the small gap between the roof-canvas and the top of one of the huge tent-poles, beyond which was the night.

"AAAAaaaahh!" a great gasp of astonishment rose up from the entire audience.

Police Inspector Purvis had been mistaken when he had told his constable that a vampire can only change into its bat-form after midnight. The truth of the matter being, as any self-respecting vampire will tell you, that he is able to transform himself into his furry, black-winged self from the moment that the first evening star appears in the sky.

It was in that split second that Count Alucard had found himself plunging groundwards, that the Count had glimpsed, through the roof of the big top, the first star of evening twinkling in the heavens. In that same split-second too, he had had the presence of mind to change himself into his vegetarian fruit-bat shape and take off, upwards, on beating wing, before he hit the floor of the circus ring. It was also in that self-same moment that the audience had given vent to its loud, astonished gasp:

"AAAAaaaahh!"

Then, before anyone inside the big top had time to comprehend what was happening, Count Alucard, the vegetarian vampire, had crept on on his bat-claws through the gap into the night.

"He's getting away again!" howled the Police Inspector, being the first one to assess the situation. "Move, lads! Everybody outside, at the double, and see if you can spot him in the helicopters' searchlights!"

Upon this command, all of the policemen turned and scurried out of the circus ring towards the exits. All of the policemen, that is to say, except for one.

Constable Hardisty was still up at the top of the rope-ladder. He was clinging tightly with both of his hands and trembling violently, having given in at last to his own fear of heights. He was trembling so much, in fact, that his Christmas Cracker paper hat had been shaken from off his head. The young copper gulped, then swallowed hard, as he watched the hat grow smaller and smaller as it floated gently down towards the sea of upturned faces below. Several moments passed before Sefton Hardisty was able to recover himself sufficiently to begin his long descent down the ladder and then set off in search of the squad.

Outside the big top, Hardisty was not at all surprised to discover confusion reigning yet again. From overhead there came a constant roaring from the helicopters which were hanging low in the night sky, scudding back and forth as they patrolled the circus area and the bushes and the flower beds of Peggotty Park beyond. On the ground, the policemen stumbled this way and that, temporarily blinded by the bright beams of the revolving searchlights underneath the helicopters, in and out of the caravans and shrubbery, falling over each other sometimes and sometimes, even, falling over their own feet. In the centre of this melee, Police Inspector Purvis stood barking orders which conflicted with orders he had barked only moments before, or issuing instructions that made neither sense nor reason to any of his men. But of the vampire, either in human or in bat-form, there was neither sight nor sign.

"Same old story," sighed Constable Hardisty to himself as he took in the situation. "Just one disaster after another."

"Don't just stand there like a baby that's lost its rattle, Hardisty!" thundered Purvis, catching sight of the young policeman. "Make yourself useful, laddie! Poke about in those thick bushes with a stick or something." And then: "No, don't do that," the Inspector continued as Hardisty moved to comply with the order. "Go down to the main gates of the park and set up a road-block. I want every vehicle thoroughly searched before it leaves."

"I suppose that someday he'll get *something* right," muttered Hardisty to himself, as he trudged off into a wooded area of the park, away from his milling companions. "But goodness only knows when that will be."

Then, realising that he was by himself in a lonely

160

part of the parkland which was sheltered from the helicopters' probing searchlights by the overhanging evergreen branches – just the sort of spot, he told himself, that a vampire might choose to skulk in – he dismissed Inspector Purvis from his mind and concentrated on his own situation.

There was some slight rustling in the nearby undergrowth caused, no doubt, by a small nocturnal creature scuttling through decaying undergrowth – but you could never be *too* sure . . . An owl hooted right over his head, causing him to jump. He would have liked to have been able to whistle a merry tune, in order to keep his spirits up, but his mouth was much too dry to allow any sound to come out of his lips.

"Well!" observed Emily Hollins, as she walked along with Albert, Henry and Jamie, "You can't say that we didn't get our money's worth tonight."

They were moving, in a steady stream of departing circus patrons, with the warm glow of the big top's open tent doors at their backs, towards the car park. The evening's entertainment, after the policemen's interruption, had resumed so smoothly, that no one in the audience had any inkling that anything untoward had taken place. No one, that is to say, except for Henry Hollins.

"Oh aye!" enthused the Scottish juggernaut driver. "It was a bonny show the nicht and nae mistake! Particularly when that fellow who was doing all the shouting got all that water squirted in his face and then had confetti flung aw' over him!"

"Yes, yes, yes!" chortled Albert Hollins, savouring the memory. "Or how about when that young man, in constable's uniform, climbed all the way up that rope-ladder and then his hat fell off!"

"I liked the exciting bits the best," opined Emily. "Like when that funny clown fell off the trapeze and everyone thought that he was going to crash to the ground – and then he suddenly shrank and changed into a bird."

"I think it was supposed to be a bat, Emily," said Albert, knowingly. "And he didn't *really* change into anything, you know. It must have been some sort of magic trick – I think it's done with mirrors. It must have been some sort of electronic plastic bat."

"I don't care what it was, Albert," replied Emily with a shiver. "It certainly put the wind up me!"

"Whatever it was, or however they did it," put in Jamie McPherson, "I'm awfu' glad we went. I've had a whale of a time. What's your opinion, Henry?"

But Henry Hollins, it appeared, did not have an opinion. He shook his head. He had remained silent during all of the conversation, walking between his parents and deep in thought. The hunt for the vampire, he realised, was over. There was no sign now of any of the policemen. They must have either caught Count Alucard or else he must have made good his escape. For a few brief minutes, in his front row circus seat, Henry had caught a glimpse of his long-lost friend, Count Alucard, and now he felt sure that he would not set eyes on him again.

They had, by this time, arrived at the car park and were standing in the shadow of Mr McPherson's juggernaut. The Scotsman clambered up onto the running-board on the passenger side, unlocked the door, opened it, and then dropped down to the ground again.

"You first, young feller-me-lad," said Jamie McPherson, taking a grip on Henry's midriff with both hands and swinging him up, easily, onto the running-board.

Henry Hollins paused, peering into the dark of the juggernaut's cab. He had been startled at the sight of someone sitting hunched on the cab's bench seat, its head in its hands. The figure raised its eyes and stared back at Henry, more surprised at seeing the boy, it seemed, than Henry had been surprised at seeing the man.

"Hello, Count Alucard," said Henry Hollins.

"Henry!" gasped the Count. "My dear, dear friend. Can it be? Fancy bumping into you."

# 10

"But how did you know where to find me?" Henry asked the Count, minutes later, when they were all five sitting in the dark, in a row, in the juggernaut's cab, and after the true situation had been explained to Albert and Emily Hollins and Jamie McPherson.

"I didn't," said the Count. "I was desperate for a place to hide, the window of this vehicle had been left partly open and so I crept inside. I had not the faintest idea, dear boy, that it had anything to do with you."

"Brilliant!" said Henry Hollins. "I've been trying to get to London for days now, to look for you."

"You didn't say anything to us about wanting to go to London to try to find somebody, Henry," chided Emily. "You said you wanted to go so you could see the Christmas tree in Trafalgar Square and Oxford Street with its Christmas lights on."

"You wouldn't have taken me to London, Mum, if you'd known the real reason why I wanted to go," said Henry then, pressing home his argument, he spoke more firmly: "In any case, he isn't just a 'somebody', he's Count Alucard. He's my friend. You met him once."

Which was quite true. Albert and Emily Hollins

had made Count Alucard's acquaintance on a previous occasion when they had been on a camping holiday in Europe (see *The Last Vampire*). But both Emily and Albert had now failed to recognise the Transylvanian nobleman behind the clown's make-up and inside the ill-fitting clown's clothing. They had, in fact, as Henry was quick to remind them, gone out of their way to show kindness to him on their first meeting, having helped him to flee from a band of hot-headed peasants who, armed with scythes and sticks and stones, had thirsted for his blood.

"That's all very well, Henry," said Mr Hollins. "But what we get up to on our holidays and how we behave when we're at home are two entirely different things. If, as you say, the Count is wanted by the police and we were to help him to escape, we would be breaking the law ourselves."

"What your father says is true, Henry," sighed the Count, his long fingers fluttering despairingly in front of his face as he continued: "Perhaps it would be best for all concerned if I were to go to the police and give myself up."

"Give yourself up for what?" demanded Henry, angrily. "You haven't done anything wrong."

"Zognar grugwor zarnog razgon," the Count said softly, giving a hopeless little shrug.

"Come again, Count?" said Emily Hollins, adding: "I didn't quite catch what you said?"

"Forgive me, dear lady," murmured Count Alucard. "It is an old saying from my native province. In your language, it means: 'A father's crimes must be paid for by his son'."

"But that's not fair!" blurted Henry. "And it's *supposed* to be Christmas," he added, although no one, including himself, could understand what that had got to do with the situation.

Emily and Albert Hollins exchanged a quick glance. They both felt sorry for the Transylvanian vegetarian vampire Count, but it seemed that they had little to offer but sympathy.

"You see, Henry," said Emily, "even if we wanted to help your friend, we're hardly in a position to do so – this isn't our juggernaut, for a start – and we can't ask Mr McPherson to involve himself in something that doesn't concern him."

Jamie McPherson, who had sat in attentive silence during all of this, drummed his fingers on the huge steering wheel and spoke up at last. "Mr and Mrs Hollins, you've been awfu' kind to me, the both of you – you've invited me intae y'r home, you've given me cups of tea and ginger nuts, aye, and treated me to an evening at the circus that I don't think I shall ever forget. What can I say? Your friends are my friends. . . ." Then, turning to Count Alucard, he added: "Whereabouts were you wanting to go?"

"I don't really care," sighed the vegetarian vampire Count then, glancing down at his ill-fitting clown's clothing, he continued: "the police can't be very far away – I daren't show myself in these parts dressed like this." Pausing, the Count nodded out of the window at where, off in the distance, the two helicopters were still patrolling the night sky, buzzing back and forth like a pair of angry wasps. "And I can't transform myself back into a bat for

166

fear of those dreadful contraptions."

"You could stay at our house," said Henry Hollins. "We could hide you up in the attic."

"A thousand thanks, my dear young friend, but sadly I must decline your generous hospitality," the Count spoke with a sad smile as he shook his head. "Supposing there was a house-to-house search?" Then, turning back to Jamie McPherson, he said: "It doesn't really matter where I go – but away from here would be an excellent beginning."

"Then say nae more, mon – you're as good as gone!"

"Before we set off," said Emily, as the juggernaut driver leaned forward to start up his engine. "Can I ask a question?"

"Aye – ask away, lassie," said Jamie McPherson.

"Is it only me?" said Emily. "Or can anybody else smell a funny smell?"

"Now that you come to mention it, Emily," said Albert, wrinkling his nose and sniffing, "I had chanced to notice a rather odd aroma, only I didn't want to be the first to mention it. A sort of doggy pong."

"Ah!" said Count Alucard. I think I may be able to shed some light on that particular odour." But before he could continue, the 'doggy pong' revealed itself. Carlos, the retired circus wolf, stuck out his head from underneath the seat. "I'm afraid I put him under there," the Count continued. "He's rather old and very lonely."

Jamie McPherson's eyes widened in alarm and he gulped at the sight of the battle-scarred veteran

wolf, Carlos, sheltering in his vehicle. Emily, however, mistaking Carlos for a more domestic brand
of animal, put out a friendly hand.

"Good doggie," said Emily, scratching Carlos on
the top of his greying head. "Who's a *good* doggie
den? *Yes*, you are! You're a good doggie, aren't
you?" And Carlos, unused to such treatment from
human strangers, growled his appreciation.

"I couldn't bear the thought of leaving him
behind," explained the Count. "He's quite harmless and very friendly."

"Nae harm done, mon," said the much-relieved
Mr McPherson then, winding down the window
to let out the animal smell, he added: "The more
the merrier, as my auld grannie used to say in
Kirkaldy."

With which, and after giving Albert Hollins a
wink, the Scotsman switched on the juggernaut's

engine and the massive vehicle shuddered into life. Then, releasing the brakes, he eased the vehicle forward and towards the car park's exit.

Count Alucard turned his eyes towards the window for a second time and was relieved to see that the helicopters, while still making their broad sweeps across the sky, seemed to be moving further away. With any luck, he told himself, the juggernaut would soon be on the open road and he would be headed towards freedom.

"Hoots, mon!" Jamie McPherson let out a mild Scottish oath as the flashlight beam struck him full in the face, blinding him temporarily and forcing him to jam his foot on the brake.

"We're sunk!" murmured Albert Hollins, gloomily. "It's a police road-block."

They had travelled barely half a kilometre when, arriving at the park's main gates, Police Inspector Purvis himself had stepped out into the path of the oncoming vehicle and shone his torch up at the windscreen, dazzling the cab's occupants.

"Stop!"

Count Alucard, his hopes of freedom shattered, ducked his head below the level of the dashboard. Henry Hollins, by screwing up his eyes, managed to peer beyond the bright beam of light and could just make out three constables standing behind the Inspector. Purvis, having despatched most of his force into the town centre, had retained this chosen hand-picked trio to man the road-block at the park's main exit.

Albert, Emily and Henry Hollins, Jamie Mc-Pherson and the cowering Count Alucard, all held their breaths while Carlos cringed beneath the seat, whimpering, as Police Inspector Purvis crossed to the side of the cab and glowered up at the window which Jamie McPherson had wound down.

"What's your name?" demanded the police officer, shining his torch up into Mr McPherson's face.

"Jamie McPherson, sor," answered the Scot, trying his best not to sound as nervous as he was feeling.

"And who are those people up there with you?"

"Friends of mine," answered Mr McPherson, truthfully.

"McWhinney's World Famous Haggis, eh?" continued Purvis, flashing his torch along the juggernaut's length. "Is that what you are carrying?"

"Aye – that it is," said Jamie McPherson, with a fierce Scots pride. "The finest haggis in the world – bar none!"

"Then perhaps you'll kindly explain to me just what, precisely, a juggernaut loaded with Scottish haggis is doing in Peggotty Park, Staplewood, at this time of night?"

"I'm on my way frae Leith tae London – and I thought I'd break my journey for a wee while. I need to have my wits about me in the morning. I've an important delivery to make to Buckingham Palace."

"Oh, yes?" sneered the Inspector. "A likely story! And I'm on my way to the Taj Mahal to join the Indian Secret Service!"

"It could be true, Inspector, what he says," proffered one of the policeman – the chubby constable with steel-rimmed glasses. "It says 'By Royal Appointment' on the side of the vehicle."

"I know that, Grimshaw!" snapped Inspector Purvis. "I'm not blind, lad."

Truth to tell though, until Constable Grimshaw had pointed it out to him, Inspector Purvis had been unaware of the important gold-lettering and the coat-of-arms on the juggernaut's side. Now that he realised that the Scotsman had been telling him the truth, the police officer was suddenly polite – or, at least, as close to politeness as he ever came.

"Oh, all right then," he grumbled up at Jamie McPherson. "I believe you – thousands wouldn't. But don't let me ever catch you loitering in a public park with this vehicle again. Get on your way, and sharp's the word, before I change my mind."

Inspector Purvis took a backward step to allow the juggernaut to proceed but before Mr McPherson could restart his vehicle, an unearthly sound rent the night air.

"Ah-whoooOOOooo . . ."

Carlos, cramped uncomfortably underneath the juggernaut's seat, had scented nervousness from his human companions and had let out the howl in sympathy for them. The fact that he had given vent to it in the close confines of the juggernaut's cab had caused it to sound so unearthly.

"What was that?" gasped Inspector Purvis, all a tremble, while his three constables moved closer to one another, each one taking comfort from the presence of the other two.

171

"What was what?" said Jamie McPherson, with wide-eyed innocence. "I didn't hear anything."

"Yes, you did. You must have done. It sounded like a . . . like a . . ." Inspector Purvis searched the back of his mind for the right word to describe the hideous sound.

"Like a werewolf, sir?" suggested Constable Grimshaw who was fond of watching late-night horror movies on the telly.

"Yes! *Yes!*" cried Purvis, with a shiver. "That's *exactly* what it sounded like. Like a horrible hairy werewolf with dripping fangs and stary luminous green eyes! First it was vampires and now it's werewolves. And, what's more, McPherson, it sounded as if it came from out of your cab."

"Not at all," said the Scotsman, nervously. "If there was a werewolf in here with us, we'd know about it. And there isn't, is there?"

"No," agreed the Hollins family, shaking their heads in unison.

"There's nobody in here but us," added Emily.

"We'll soon see about that," said Inspector Purvis, staring up at the juggernaut's door, but hesitant about approaching it for fear of the dreadful creature that might be contained within. "Hardisty!"

"Sir?"

"Take this," said Purvis, tossing his flashlight to the young policeman. "Get up there and give that cab a thorough inspection."

"*Me*, sir?" said Hardisty, aghast.

"Yes, laddie! You heard. Get on with it. We can't hang about here all night."

172

"Why does it always have to be me that gets the awkward jobs," wondered Sefton Hardisty bitterly as he approached the juggernaut's cab. Good Lord above, he'd already chased a vampire up a swaying rope-ladder *and* walked all by himself through a lonely wood with hooting owls and furry creatures scurrying in the undergrowth. Hadn't he done enough for one night? Supposing there *was* a were-wolf in the driver's cab? He wouldn't stand a chance. It would have its slavering fangs inside his neck the moment that he poked his head inside the window. Crikey! Constable Sefton Hardisty's hand was shaking as he reached up to gain a handhold before hauling himself up level with the open window.

Had Hardisty but known it though, the several occupants of the juggernaut's cab were all as fright-ened as he was himself. The game, it seemed to them, was up. The Count's presence was about to be discovered – and then they would all end up in serious trouble. . . . Constable Hardisty's head appeared silhouetted at the open window. His torch beam swept the inside of the cab and the several occupants blinked in its bright light.

The torch was shaking slightly in the young policeman's hand as the thin bright beam of light played on the faces, one by one. The juggernaut's driver first, then a couple sitting close together, and then a boy who looked about eleven years of age.

"Good-oh!" thought Hardisty, relieved. "No sign of a vampire *or* a werewolf so far!"

But the constable seemed to feel his heart leap

into his mouth as the pencil-thin beam of light picked out another figure sitting glumly in the cab. It was a thin-faced man in a black ill-fitting suit, his dark, beady eyes accentuated by the white clown make-up he was wearing. Hardisty recognised the figure instantly. He had every reason to! It was the same long-limbed man that he himself had pursued to dizzy heights up the swaying rope-ladder, only to lose at the very moment that he had seemed to have him! It was the vampire himself!

More than that though, peering out from between the vampire's legs was a cowering creature mostly concealed beneath the juggernaut's seat – an animal with luminous green unblinking eyes and slobbering jowls. It was the werewolf!

"Oh, crumbs!" Hardisty told himself. "I've come across not one monster but a pair of them!"

The young constable's first instinct was to yell out at the top of his voice. The only thing that prevented him from doing just that was the fact that his mouth had suddenly gone dry with fright. Then, in the short time that it took for him to run his tongue around the inside of his cheeks and gums, moistening them, the young policeman had a sudden change of heart.

Looking into the vampire's frightened eyes, the young policeman felt himself engulfed in a wave of pity for the sad creature. After all, he asked himself, what crimes exactly had the so-called monster committed? None at all, so far as Hardisty was aware. He only had Inspector Purvis's word on that account and, as Constable Hardisty knew full well, his superior officer had a habit of getting things

wrong more times than he got them right. As for the werewolf – well, on second glance it occurred to Hardisty that the animal's eyes weren't luminous after all – that had been a trick of the torch-light. Neither could it be said that its jowls were really slobbering. . . . The wolf, if wolf it was, was panting, yes – but was it panting for human blood, he had to ask himself? Or was it panting simply because it was frightened? Besides, if it *was* a wolf – weren't wolves, like bats, a protected species . . .?

"What's happening up there, Hardisty?" Inspector Purvis called up in a peevish voice from the ground below. "What's in there, laddie? Is there a vampire or a werewolf? Come on, Hardisty! Out with it! Don't just stand there dithering!"

Sefton Hardisty had to make a quick decision

and he did just that. "There's nothing in here, sir!" called the young policeman in a clear, firm voice. "Nothing except Mr McPherson and his friends." Which, after all, was nothing less than the truth.

"Are you *sure* about that, laddie?" the Police Inspector called back, sounding disappointed.

"Oh, absolutely, sir!" replied Hardisty, switching off his torch and returning the cab's occupants into the safe custody of darkness, then: "Good luck!" he whispered into that dark. "I hope you get away." He paused, then added: "Have a Happy Christmas!" With which, the young constable leaped down from the running-board onto the ground.

Moments later, after Inspector Purvis had waved the juggernaut reluctantly on, the vehicle picked up speed and turned left out of the park's main gates and onto the road beyond.

"Where are ye headed now?" asked Jamie McPherson of Count Alucard as soon as they had put a safe distance between the juggernaut and the police.

"Who knows?" sighed the Count, with a shrug of his thin shoulders accompanied by an eloquent fluttering of his long fingers. "I think I should leave England for a while at least. If you could drop me somewhere near a river, I could follow it, flying by night, and find the coastline. That would be a start." He paused, then added: "I think I might try and find my way back home – to Transylvania."

"Transylvania?" said the Scotsman, taking his eyes off the road ahead just long enough to give the Count a curious glance. "Why – there's a coincidence if ever I heard tell o' one. I'm going to

Transylvania ma'sel', mon."

"You're going to Transylvania?" echoed the astonished Count.

"That I am – as soon as I've made my Buckingham Palace delivery tomorrow morning, ah'm headed for the cross-Channel ferry. I've a brace o'prime haggis to deliver in a town called Tolokovin."

"Tolokovin?" The Count sounded more bemused than ever. "That's hardly a stone's throw from the ruins of Castle Alucard. I left my most comfortable coffin in an underground dungeon in those ruins. I do hope that it hasn't been vandalised."

"But if you're going to Transylvania, Mr McPherson," put in Henry Hollins, "won't it take days and days?"

"Aye, laddie – days and days and then some, there and back," agreed the juggernaut driver.

"Then you won't be home in time for Christmas, will you?" said Henry.

"Nay, I will not," said Jamie McPherson. "It's a worthwhile and satisfying career I've carved out for ma'sel' – delivering the world's finest haggis all over Europe . . ." he paused and then added softly, "aye, but mon, it's also a very lonely one."

"Perhaps, dear friend, the road would not seem quite so long this Christmas," said Count Alucard, "if you were to allow me to share the journey with you?"

"I was about to suggest that very same thing!" said Jamie McPherson, smiling broadly.

"But what about the doggie?" ventured Emily,

nodding at the old wolf.

"I have yet to take a decision on his account, dear lady," said the vegetarian vampire nobleman.

Carlos was something of a problem. The Count did not believe that the old wolf's future lay in Transylvania. The Middle European winters would surely prove too harsh for the old wolf after all of the years spent in captivity. On the other hand, the Count had no intention of leaving Carlos behind in England without first finding him a suitable home – one where he would have space to roam and yet not be lonely. . . . It was a vexing problem and one to which Count Alucard could see no easy solution.

Happily, and unknown to the Count, it was a problem which would soon resolve itself.

# 11

"Halt! Who goes there – friend or foe?" called Scots Guardsman Dougal McGreevy, pointing his rifle up at the cab of the juggernaut which had just drawn up on the forecourt of Buckingham Palace.

"Friend!" yelled down Jamie McPherson, through the open window of his driving cab. "It's the Keeper o' the Royal Haggis, Dougal! I would ha' thought ye knew me well enough after all these years, mon, not to ask silly questions!"

"Ah'm awfu' sorry, Jamie," said the sentry. "I ken *you* fine – but it's aw' the folk that ye' have wi' ye in y're vehicle that I'm concerned about?"

Upon which, Albert Hollins cleared his throat and announced his own identity in a loud, clear voice: "The Keeper of the Royal Garden Gnomes, his immediate family and a friend," he cried, inventing a title for himself and, at the same time, holding up the case containing the two gnomes which had been resting on his lap.

"Advance, Keeper of the Royal Garden Gnomes, family and friend, and be recognised!" commanded the sentry, pointing his rifle challengingly.

Albert, Emily and Henry Hollins, Count Alucard with Carlos panting at his side, and Jamie

McPherson bringing up the rear, clambered down from the juggernaut's cab then stamped their feet and stretched their legs while Guardsman McGreevy cast his soldier's expert eye over them. It was a cold, clear morning not long after dawn; there was little traffic along The Mall and, as yet, no sign outside the Palace railings of eager early-morning tourists.

Jamie McPherson, his juggernaut and its passengers, after driving away from Peggotty Park on the previous night, had paused at 42, Nicholas Nickleby Close, long enough to collect the garden gnomes, eat a quick snack – and then, a little while longer for Emily to take a decision about the clothes that she would wear for her trip to Buckingham Palace.

"I really should choose something extra-special," she had pondered, presenting herself in a change of clothing for the umpteenth time, in front of her family and guests, in the living-room of her home. "Supposing I should chance to bump into the Queen or the Duke of Edinburgh?"

"Ye'll nae do that, lassie," Jamie McPherson had explained to Emily, for his frequent deliveries to the Palace had made him something of an expert on court protocol. "The entire Royal Family caboodle are awa' on holiday at Christmastime."

All the same, once they had put Staplewood behind them and had driven through the night, Emily had insisted on another stop along the way, lasting several hours, at a motorway service station, in order to prepare herself in the ladies toilets, for her important visit. During which time, Jamie

McPherson, Albert and Henry Hollins had enjoyed a pre-dawn breakfast of sausages, bacon, eggs, grilled tomatoes, brown toast, marmalade in individual pots and hot sweet tea, while Count Alucard had dined on fresh fruit salad and freshly squeezed orange juice. Neither had Carlos been forgotten, for although they had been forced to leave him in the juggernaut's cab, both the Count and Henry had made trips out onto the car park, taking choice hamburgers to the old wolf.

Now, as they stamped their feet and blew on their hands in the chill morning air in the Palace forecourt, the Hollinses, the juggernaut driver, Count Alucard, even Carlos the wolf, were all grateful that they had paused to refresh themselves at the motorway service station. Dougal McGreevy, the Palace sentry, still unsure as to how many of the visitors should be allowed entry to the Palace itself, was keeping them hanging about far longer than seemed necessary.

"Away wi' ye, Dougal McGreevy!" snapped Jamie McPherson, impatiently. "Ah was delivering McWhinney's haggis here before you were even born, boy. Ah come and go as ah please, mon – I always have done and ah always will!"

"*You* can proceed wi' those, Jamie," allowed the sentry, nodding at the half-dozen family-size haggis which the juggernaut driver carried in his arms. "Aye – an' that gentleman can go in too, wi' his delivery," he continued, indicating Mr Hollins who had the case containing the garden gnomes tucked safely under one arm. "An' the lady and the laddie may go wi' him, if ye say they're his immediate family. But I dinna ha' the authority to let *every* Tom, Dick or Harry go past," he concluded, looking at the sorry sight of Count Alucard in his ill-fitting suit of clown's borrowed clothing with the mangy-looking Carlos at his heel.

"Why, mon, he's a fully-fledged member o' the Transylvanian aristocracy!" stormed Jamie McPherson. "He's more right to go intae yon Palace than any of us – and if Her Majesty was in residence, she'd have nipped out here to tell ye so hersel'."

"Please, dear friend," murmured the Count to Mr McPherson, not wishing to cause a fuss. "I do beg of you, do not distress yourself. I am more than happy to wait out here in the courtyard until you have completed your business – it is a matter of little importance—"

"On the contrary – it is a matter of *great* importance," broke in a quavering voice from behind their backs. They all turned and looked at the slightly stooping figure of the silvery-haired elderly manservant, in the black trousers, polished black shoes, white wing-collar shirt and neat black tie, with a green-baize butler's apron tied around his middle. "In the absence of Her Majesty, sentry," he went on, "I will authorise his right of way."

"Oh, well," demurred the sentry, lowering his rifle at last, "if he's got your permission to pass, Mr Yakov, who am I tae argue."

"Yakov?" exclaimed Count Alucard, staring into the wrinkled face of the old gentleman who had just come out of the Palace. "*Yakov* – the same dear, good Yakov of my childhood? Can it really be you?"

183

"The very same, sir," murmured the butler, as surprised at seeing the Count as the Count was to set eyes on him. "Yakov – the manservant who was in your father's employ all those many years ago."

Both close to tears, the two men embraced each other warmly while Henry Hollins, his parents, Jamie McPherson and Guardsman Dougal McGreevy looked on in silence.

"Will that be all you'll be wanting, Mr Yakov?" asked Millie Mosscrop, the Buckingham Palace kitchen maid, placing a silver tray containing a matching monogrammed silver teapot, milk jug, sugar bowl and fine bone china cups and saucers on the kitchen table for the butler and his guests.

"Thank you, Millie," said the old butler, gravely. "You are most kind."

Millie, who was wearing a black frock, a white apron, a white lace-trimmed cap with two white ribbons dangling down the back, white ankle socks and trainers, bobbed a curtsey at Mr Yakov, then winked at Henry Hollins before skipping out of the kitchen.

"But where have you been all these long years, Yakov?" asked Count Alucard as the old butler poured out tea for the Hollins family, Jamie Mc-Pherson and the Count himself, who were all grouped around the well-scrubbed table, enjoying the warmth of the Palace kitchen.

"After the Castle Alucard was ransacked and burned to the ground, sir, I took refuge with the other servants in the mountain caves for all of that summer – when autumn came I moved on, seeking employment around the palaces of Europe. I arrived in the United Kingdom several years ago and, with regard to my considerable experience, was fortunate enough to gain a position here."

"But the Castle Alucard was rebuilt, Yakov," said the Count, as the aged butler handed him his cup of tea.

"I was not to know that, sir."

"Rebuilt," repeated Count Alucard, softly, sadly

185

and half to himself, "then ransacked and burned down again, several times over many years."

"I say!" cried Emily Hollins, breaking the silence which followed and swivelling her teacup in its saucer in order to admire the picture of Windsor Castle with which it was embellished. "These are posh and no mistake!"

"But what about yourself, sir?" asked Yakov, his eyes straying over the well-worn, ill-fitting suit the Count was wearing. "I hardly feel it is for me to ask, sir, but have you fallen upon hard times?"

"There are good times and there are bad times, Yakov, for all of us," said the Count wryly, looking down in some slight embarrassment at where his long thin wrists poked out of the too-short sleeves of his jacket. "Times are never too harsh though," he added, smiling at Henry Hollins, "when a man has friends that he may count upon."

"If I might make so bold, sir, it would seem to me that you are about the same height and slim proportions as was His Royal Highness, my employer, when he was a younger man. I am sure that I could lay my hands on a suit for which His Royal Highness has no further use and which you might care to borrow as a temporary stopgap."

"And which I would be only to pleased to return with my grateful thanks, Yakov," replied Count Alucard overjoyed. "As soon as I have been able to arrange a meeting with Grigor Yavtukesh, my tailor in Tolokovin, and had him measure me up for a new suit. But are you sure that your master, His Royal Highness, will have no objection to my borrowing his clothes?"

"On the contrary, sir," replied old Yakov, inclining his head. "Had he been in residence, and not on Christmas holiday, I am sure that he would have proposed the very same solution himself."

"Speaking o' Tolokovin," said Jamie McPherson, his cup poised between the saucer and his lips, his little finger delicately crooked, befitting his surroundings, "Ah've nae wish to rush anybody – but if we *are* tae catch the cross channel ferry, *and* drop Emily, Albert and young Henry here, at their hotel, we shall need ta shift oursel's."

"In which case," said Albert Hollins, rising to his feet and picking up the two garden gnomes which he had previously taken out of their packaging, "I would like to pop out into the Palace gardens, and find a suitable home for these two chappies. Unless, of course," he added hastily, turning to old Yakov, "it is a task more suited to the royal gardeners?"

"Please, Mr Hollins," said Yakov, extending both his hands, palms upward, "no one is better fitted than yourself to find the correct location for those delightful figures – after all, you are the expert in the world of garden gnomes."

Albert Hollins, pleased by the compliment, was whistling cheerfully as he strolled out of the kitchen with a garden gnome tucked under each arm. Emily, who was never happier than when she was togged out in her green wellies and her gardening gloves, was quick to follow her husband. She was eager to discover whether the Royal Family's London garden was a match for her own neat patch at the back of 42, Nicholas Nickleby Close.

"My stars!" gulped Emily, as she caught her first glimpse of the wide lawns, neat flower beds waiting for the warmth of spring, and giving way to the clumps of evergreens and little copses beyond. "You would never dream they had so much garden," she gasped, "when you look at the Palace from the front."

Adding to this delightful scene, was the sight of Carlos, who had whined to be let out some minutes before, excitedly pounding round and round the lawn, in ever-decreasing circles, with a frisky corgi playfully snapping and yapping at his heels.

"Well!" laughed Emily, watching the old wolf. "He seems to be enjoying himself and no mistake!"

"He's not the only one," said Albert, as Carlos came to a sudden stop, rolled onto his back, waved his legs in the air and thumped his tail on the ground while the corgi tumbled all over him delightedly.

"That's Maggie," said the butler, nodding at the corgi. "She had to stay behind when the other corgis went off on holiday with their Royal Highnesses. She had been unwell and the Royal Vet confined her to her kennel. But she seems much better at having found a new friend," he added as the small dog and the old wolf resumed their hectic race around the lawn.

"A cunning old fellow like Carlos," mused Count Alucard, who had also come out of the Palace and was gazing out towards the wooded area beyond the formal lawns and flower beds, "could make a home down there without anyone barely noticing that he was about." He paused, rubbed

thoughtfully at his chin with a pale slim hand, then turned to Yakov who was standing at his side. "I don't suppose, old friend," he murmured tentatively, "that you might see your way to leaving out some late-night kitchen scraps?"

"It would be more than a pleasure, sir, it would be my delight," said the butler. "In the old days, if you will cast your mind back to your childhood, it was I who took it upon myself to see that the forest wolf-pack did not go hungry when the winter snows lay thick upon the ground. I would also point out, sir, that the kitchen scraps at this residence are the equal of those anywhere in the world – particularly when we have had diplomats or crowned heads to dinner."

"That settles that then," said Henry Hollins, grinning up at the Count.

Not much later, as the Hollinses, Jamie McPherson and Count Alucard moved off in the direction of the forecourt where they had left the juggernaut, Henry cast a last glance back over his shoulder and caught sight of old Yakov bending down to ruffle the fur at the back of Carlos's head, while the old wolf's jaws were snapping at a sizeable titbit. From that distance, Henry Hollins could not quite make out just what it was that the butler had given to his animal friend, but it looked to be similar in colour, size and shape to a family-size McWhinney's World Famous Haggis.

"Eat up, Carlos," murmured Henry Hollins softly and to himself. "Enjoy your food."

"London is all very well," opined Emily Hollins, opening a storage tin and taking out six of her own home-baked mince pies, "but when it comes to the nitty-gritty, there's no place like home at Christmastime."

It was Christmas Eve and the Hollins family, having spent their two-day jaunt in London, enjoying both the busy shops and the sightseeing, were back safely home at 42, Nicholas Nickleby Close, preparing themselves for the next few days' festivities. There would be roast turkey for the next day's lunch, with chipolata sausages, sage-and-onion stuffing, roast potatoes and several kinds of vegetables. What's more, there would be Christmas pudding to follow. There were presents piled under the Christmas tree to be unwrapped in the morning and Henry would wake to his own pillow case full of surprises at the end of his bed. He was a little sad that he would not be seeing his friend, Count Alucard, over the holiday but he took comfort in the fact that the vegetarian vampire Count would be back in his native Transylvania on Christmas Day.

"Mum's right," Henry told himself, "there is no place like home at Christmas."

"Now then," said Emily Hollins, as she popped her half-dozen mince pies onto a baking tray and switched on the oven. "There are hot mince pies for tea," she announced. "Who wants theirs with ice-cream, and who wants brandy butter?"

"Decisions, decisions," murmured Albert Hollins, jokingly, as he poured out seasonal glasses of ginger wine.

"I dinna ken which road to take – I think we're lost, the noo," admitted Jamie McPherson, trying to peer through the snow flakes which were falling thick and fast in the juggernaut's headlights, and into the dark night of the pine forest which lay beyond.

"Take heart – Tolokovin cannot be far from here," said Count Alucard, sitting at the juggernaut driver's side, resplendent in his borrowed Buckingham Palace clothing.

In addition to the well-cut smart black jacket and trousers, old Yakov had also kindly loaned the Count a starched white shirt, a black bow tie, some socks, a pair of highly polished patent-leather shoes and some fine silk polka-dotted underpants bearing the monogram, 'H.R.H.'. To complete the outfit, the Count had also borrowed a black opera cloak with a red satin lining. It was his intention, of course, to return all of these items back where they belonged at the earliest opportunity. For the time being though, with all thanks due to Buckingham Palace, the Count considered himself as well turned out as he had been for many a long Transylvanian moon.

"What a way tae spend Christmas Eve," sighed Jamie McPherson, as the snow seemed to come down even faster.

They had pulled up at a cross-roads. At some time, there must have been a signpost to point out the way, but it had long since fallen down. They were left with three roads to choose from, but a wrong decision could leave them stranded, in deep snow, somewhere in the forest which stretched for mile after mile in every direction.

"There are times when it is good to be a vampire," said Count Alucard, adding: "Wait – and watch."

With which, the Count swung open the door, letting in the cold and some swirling snow flakes, stepped out onto the running-board and then up onto the vehicle's bonnet. He stood for a moment, his arms outstretched, his long thin fingers clutching at the hem of his cloak. Then, to Jamie McPherson's amazement, gazing through the windscreen, he again saw the Count suddenly seem to shrivel, transformed into the small, black furry creature which hovered, on parchment-like wings, above the juggernaut's bonnet.

Taking off, the Count soared high above the cross-roads and the pine trees. Far off, in the distance through the now gently falling snow, he could see the welcoming lights of Tolokovin, blinking in a break in the forest. His sharp bat's eyes could even make out the coloured lights on the Christmas tree in Tolokovin Market Square. And did his keen bat's ears deceive him, he wondered, or could he just detect the voices of a children's choir, singing an old Transylvanian Christmas carol?

> "*Rovenyi Vorovna Venrov,*
> *Venron Vorovna Venirov. . . .*"

Best of all though, hanging low in the night sky, directly over the little Transylvanian town, was a Christmas star.

Moments later, the Count was back in human

form and sitting beside Jamie McPherson in the warmth of the juggernaut's cab, brushing the last few lingering flakes of snow from his smart black suit.

"Which way do we go then?" asked the juggernaut driver.

Count Alucard nodded up above the pine trees, through the snow, into the dark night sky. "Follow that star," he said.

Jamie McPherson started up the juggernaut's engine and, once again, the massive vehicle juddered into life.

# EPILOGUE

Christmas came and went. The first snowdrops thrust their way, miraculously as always, through the cold hard earth at the farthest fringes of the Buckingham Palace gardens. Spring arrived, a little early that year, bringing with it the daffodils, the crocuses and the hyacinths. Later on, the formal flower beds were ablaze with a rich, red carpet of tulips.

The garden gnomes, which Albert Hollins had placed to their best advantage – one leaning on his shovel by the edge of a herbaceous border, the other sitting, dangling his fishing rod over the Palace fish pond – were a great success with both the Royal Family and important visitors alike.

So many were the favourable comments, in fact, that the Royal Palace became a subscriber to the Gnome of the Month Club. Garden gnomes have since appeared at every twist and turn in the Royal Palace gardens: some peering out, holding up painted lanterns, from beneath the laurel bushes; others are diligently poised in the flower beds with a fork or a hoe or a rake to hand; less active garden gnomes sit reading books in quiet shady nooks and cloisters.

In summer, when Buckingham Palace is host to royal garden parties, and the broad well-trimmed lawns are thronged with fashionable folk dressed mid-week in their Sunday best, the chit-chat is not of Ascot races, or theatrical first nights, or of summer balls – it is talk of garden gnomes that is on fashionable society's lips.

Best of all though, are the summer evenings, when the garden party crowds are gone and the last striped marquee has been taken down. Then, in the cool of late evening, when the shadows lengthen across the royal lawns, it is sometimes possible to catch a glimpse of a grey-headed, four-legged creature loping across the grass pursued by half-a-dozen corgis. Few people, of course, apart from those of royal birth, are favoured with such a pleasing sight. But if you should ever chance to walk along Buckingham Palace Road, when the moon is full, you might just chance to hear the unlikely sound of a wild animal's howl, rising and falling on the warm night air:

"Ah-WHOOO-oooo-OOOO...."